# SOULMATE

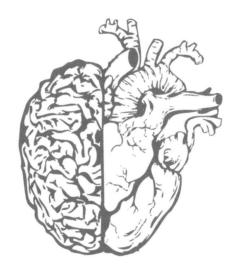

SOULMATE

TitleTown Publishing, LLC
P.O. Box 12093  Green Bay, WI  54307-12093
titletownpublishing.com


PUBLISHER'S CATALOGING-IN-PUBLICATION DATA:


Names:  Block, EL, author.
Title: Soulmate / EL Block.
Description:  Green Bay, WI : TitleTown Publishing, LLC, [2024]


Identifiers: ISBN:      978-1-955047-35-7 (hardcover)
                             978-1-955047-64-7 (eBook)


Subjects:   LCSH: Soul mates--Fiction. | Coma--Patients--Fiction. | Lucid dreams--Fiction. | Memory--Fiction. | Reality--Fiction. | Near-death experiences--Fiction. | Man-woman relationships--Fiction. | Alienation (Social psychology)--Fiction. | Change--Psychological aspects--Fiction. | Romance fiction, American. | Fate and fatalism--Fiction. | Suspense fiction. | Psychological fiction. | LCGFT: Thrillers (Fiction) | BISAC: FICTION / Thrillers / Psychological. | FICTION / Thrillers / Supernatural.

Classification: LCC: PS3602.L64263 S68 2024 | DDC: 813.6--dc23

*This story is for everyone who's missing someone they have yet to meet.*

*for Kaitlin Wiza*

"Whatever our souls are made of, his and mine are the same."
—Emily Brontë, *Wuthering Heights*

# Alaina Ryan

My father was the greatest man I had ever known, and the man by which all other men would be eternally measured. He never regarded himself as great; he was actually quite self-deprecating. He was honest, hard-working, and he genuinely cared about people. He made a career for himself in the military after high school, and met my mother while on a short leave in the Mediterranean between assignments. My mother was a beauty, and barely nineteen. He was eight years her senior. Age differences weren't as concerning in that part of the world, but my grandparents didn't love the idea of their only daughter marrying an American soldier.

My mother was equal parts naïve and genius. She wanted to do something important with her life, to make her mark on the world, despite her oppressive upbringing. I had no doubt she fell in love with my father as instantly as he did with her, but I also believed she saw in him the opportunity to escape a life she felt trapped by. She had no interest in spending her life working in her family's vineyard. She wanted to see the world, to experience all that life had to offer, and in her death, leave behind a piece of herself she could be proud of.

It was rare for anyone to see beyond the way she looked. No one was really interested in who she truly was, except for my father. He understood her, and he knew how she needed to be loved – something I never learned. She was a woman of extremes. She was often dramatic and unreasonable. I'm not sure she ever had any interest in being a mother. She seemed to find me inhibitive most of the time. She was lovely when my father was away. We would cook and garden together, make art and read books, take walks and play games. She doted on me. I was her best friend. Likely her only friend. But when my father was home, she seemed frustrated by my continued presence, and by his interest in spending time with me. Love, marriage, family, human companionship in any form, is difficult and flawed.

Whenever my father came home from an assignment, he would always say, "Returning home safely is an underrated blessing." One day, when I was twelve years old, my father didn't come home. I was devastated, of course, but my mother was completely shattered. She took all the air from the room, as she always had. My grief was forcibly muted under the gravity of her own.

My mother became ill shortly after his death and continued to decline over the next four long, grueling years. I became her caregiver and her counselor, despite my own adolescent needs. I tried with everything I had, but I could not understand her as he did. I could not love her as he did. She passed away when I was sixteen years old. I loved my mother deeply, but with her death came my own opportunity to escape a life I felt trapped by.

For the first twelve years of my life, I witnessed the most incredible love story I had ever seen between two people. I also witnessed a husband struggle to parent his temperamental wife. I watched a young woman give up on everything she wanted for herself, for her life, to be the wife and mother she never planned to be. Ultimately, their love story destroyed her. On the day of her funeral, as I took one last look at my beautiful mother before her casket was closed forever, I promised myself that I would never allow love to commandeer my life and draw me in the opposite direction of my purpose.

# Jake Matthews

My brother and I had a pretty ideal childhood. We had two loving parents who also loved each other, and that was more uncommon than it should be. My dad was a doctor, like all of the men on my father's side of the family had been. It was expected that my brother and I would become doctors as well. My mom was a nurse until she met my dad. She once told me, "While I did truly love being a nurse, most women of my generation became nurses for the express purpose of meeting and marrying a doctor. Only the spinsters made a career of it." She couldn't wait to become a wife and a mother, a homemaker, which she found to be a much more agreeable term than housewife. She loved it, and she was great at it.

My dad shared a private medical practice with a close friend. They were room-mates throughout medical school and completed their residency together at Northwestern, before deciding to use his friend's family money to open up a private practice. They hoped to one day hand it off to my brother and me, his partner deciding his only daughter was better suited to be a doctor's wife than a doctor herself. She and I were pushed together from an early age. We didn't have anything even close to what my parents had, but I convinced myself that kind of love was so rare, that most people would never find it in their lifetime anyway. What we did have made sense on paper, and for a long time, I let myself think that was enough. Love, marriage, family, human companionship in any form, is difficult and flawed.

I'd always loved nature. When I was younger, I worked at the local greenhouse every summer, and on weekends during the school year. I loved the fresh air and the physical labor. I could have been really happy as a landscaper, or a groundskeeper of some kind. All I'd ever cared about was earning an honest living and building a loving family of my own. My dad assured me that I would come to love the life he had planned for me. I wasn't sure about that, but I was sure that my children would be able to choose what kind of life they wanted to live, and who they wanted to love. I didn't want them to dread going to work – or to dread coming home. I didn't want them to feel like what they wanted for themselves wasn't good enough.

I did enjoy being a doctor, especially on the days when I was truly able to make a difference for someone. The hours were long, but they passed by quickly. My days were interesting and exhausting enough to keep my mind from constantly questioning how I'd been conceding to live my life. Most days, I was happiest in the short moments I spent completely alone, away from the hospital, my wife, and that godforsaken house.

*Caris Carlisle*

When I was a little girl, my mother tried to drown me. My father returned home from work, earlier than she expected I would have to imagine, and happened to catch her holding me underwater in the pool. I couldn't really remember it, except for a few flashing images that overtook my mind during times of stress, like pieces of a recurring nightmare. The one thing I remembered with cruel detail was her bathing suit – a chevron pattern of alternating navy blue and crisp white. I remembered the way it clung tightly to her body, and the slick feeling of the material as I frantically tried to grasp it from beneath the water's surface.

Following this incident, my father had my mother involuntarily committed. Shortly thereafter, the pool was built over. From then on, I was fragile in my father's eyes. I was all but confined to the house, and to the company of the private caregiver he'd hired. I wasn't allowed to see friends outside of school, or to attend school functions. When I reached the age of sixteen, I couldn't learn to drive, and I certainly wasn't permitted to date. Once I completed my schooling, I was promptly transferred from the caregiver into Jake's care. Following a hasty private wedding, my father gave us the house and everything inside of it that was no longer of value to him. He left his medical practice and moved to a retirement community in North Carolina. He called me every year on my birthday, at exactly the same time, for exactly one hour, just as he did with my mother in the asylum. Every early December, I received a Christmas card with a check to cover the next year's estate expenses. That was the extent of our relationship. Love, marriage, family, human companionship in any form, is difficult and flawed.

The moment I realized I was in love with Jake Matthews happened when I was just six years old. It was probably my earliest memory, and one I could never forget. My parents were hosting a party at the house, and I wasn't feeling very well. My mother was focused on her house, my father was focused on his guests, and I was meant to stay in my room. I kept creeping down the main staircase, and tried the back stairs as well, only to be spotted and shooed back upstairs by the silent upward pointing of one parent or the other. Witnessing this, Jake snuck upstairs and stayed with me, taking care of me and holding my hand until we both fell asleep. I remember waking to the sound of our fathers talking in the doorway to my bedroom.

"Well, Tom," my father inappropriately joked, "Your son has slept with my daughter, so I expect you'll see that he does right by her." Sheltered and naïve, I was a married woman before I truly understood the joke.

Jake was my soulmate, my best friend, and the love of my life. I was quite aware he had never been in love with me. I was also quite aware this was not at all the life he wanted for himself. I did my best to ignore what I knew, because I desperately wanted a life with him. This life, and every life to come. I hoped that over time his feelings for me would grow. His unwavering care and kindness often allowed me to delude myself into thinking they had.

# Part One

"The greatest use of life is to spend it on something that will outlast it."
—William James

## THURSDAY MORNING

### Alaina

I awoke at sunrise, just as I did every morning. Just as my father always had. I owed all of my good habits to my father. Somatic yoga and meditation in the garden, followed by a steam shower. I dressed comfortably for the airplane and packed a small carry-on suitcase. I would only be gone through the weekend. I wasn't one of those women who overpacked, who was comforted by having endless options at my disposal. If my work in neuroscience and quantum physics had taught me anything, it was to control as many variables as possible. I carefully orchestrated every possible aspect of my life. I strived for efficiency, and to make the most of every single day. One can never predict which day might be your last. The Roman philosopher, Seneca, supposedly once said, "Life is long enough, and it has been given in sufficiently generous measure to allow for the accomplishment of the greatest things, if the whole of it is well invested."

My work demanded a fair amount of travel, and I followed the same routine every time I left the house. A sweep of every room, even those I didn't use, to make sure everything was turned off, unplugged, and locked. I double-checked my purse for my phone, wallet, and keys. As long as I always had those three things, I was secure in an insecure world. I had a way to communicate, a way to acquire anything I might need, and a way to return home safely.

I placed my suitcase in the front passenger seat of the SUV, climbed into the driver's seat, and latched my seatbelt. I slid on my favorite large-framed Prada sunglasses, started the engine, and paused to pray – or at least what I considered praying. I spoke the same words every time. Another routine.

*Dear God, angels, and spirit guides, please watch over my home. Bless it, protect it, and keep it safe and sound while I'm away. Please surround me with the white light of the holy spirit and keep me safe as well.*

The garage door lowered behind me, and I took one last look at my childhood home in the rear view mirror before pulling onto the county road that would lead me to the White Plains airport. The radio was off, as it always was. There was rarely anything worthwhile on the radio. Driving in silence was contemplative, and a better use of my time. There were specific circumstances that called for carefully curated playlists, and others that called for audio books. The circumstances of this trip called for peace.

I'd been feeling quite unsettled since my recent twenty-fourth birthday. The anniversary of my father's death was approaching once again, and I was dreading this one even more than the years before. Being twenty-four meant that from this anniversary forward, I would have officially been living without him longer than I'd lived with him. Rationally I knew this was trivial, but emotionally it felt incredibly significant, like I was crossing some sort of imaginary line that meant I could no longer justify being this impacted and defined by his death.

My mother took to wheel throwing after my father died, turning the guest house into a pottery studio. That, and the gardens, were the only things that could soothe her soul in his absence. They were the only two things that distracted her enough while she was awake, and exhausted her enough to sleep at length, where she swore she was spending time with my father in her dreams. She simply opted out of everything else in life, including motherhood.

She headed for her pottery studio shortly after sunrise each day and worked until well past dark. I would bring her a small pot of strong black tea, and sourdough toast or a croissant with French butter, later in the morning. I checked on her in the early afternoon, then again to bring her a light dinner, and once more to say goodnight. Most days, she refused to look up from what she was working on, much less say something in acknowledgment. Sometimes I would set them down next to her and just stand there, waiting in silence. Occasionally she would quickly dart her eyes up at me, then snap them back down to her work. She knew I was standing there. She knew what I so desperately wanted from her, needed from her, and she was not about to indulge me. Such a small thing to expect from one's mother, grieving or otherwise. Sometimes I would set them down just inside the door and leave quietly, hoping not to be seen at all, hoping they would grow cold before she noticed them, and perhaps she might wonder why I had not made my presence known that day. If she ever gave a single thought to me, I had no way to know it.

The positive side effect of her obsessive artistic practice, and neglect of all else, was an incredible body of artistic work. The simple and hollow caverns, all glazed in plain French white, were a visual representation of who she had become – fragile and ghostly, yet somehow still captivatingly beautiful. When my father was alive, she was very much alive as well. She was a pastry chef. She created culinary masterpieces; delicious, sculptural works of art for others to devour and enjoy. In his absence, she turned to creating these empty vessels; thin, impermanent shells with nothing inside of them. She never signed them or titled them. It was as if she refused to take ownership of them. As each new batch was removed from the kiln and cooled completely, she carefully packed them inside rows of plain wooden crates. She stacked the crates so high they became thick walls around her, like a mausoleum of unmarked graves.

It was so difficult, as a young girl, not to take it personally that she was unable to find any joy in me, that she couldn't see my father shining through me, and treasure me as a part of him that still flourished. Instead, I seemed to have become nothing more than a constant caregiver to her broken remains, and a painful reminder of what broke her. Every day she became sicker and angrier, literally filled with rage, that she had again woken up to a reality that didn't include him.

Every once in a while, there would be a glimpse of her, and I had to be so careful not to let that glimpse become a glimmer of hope that maybe her grief had taken a turn for the better. I was lonely and grieving, too, after all. I couldn't allow the occasional smoothing of my hair, followed by a light kiss on the top of my head, or the rare French term of endearment, to become what I lived for. I refused to waste my days longing for her to return from the dead and give my life purpose, the way she did with him. She loved me, in her own way. Deep down, I knew that. But there was never a doubt in my mind that if she'd somehow been given the chance to exchange my life for his, she would have done so in a heartbeat. As the days wore on, I quietly came to terms with who she was, and how losing the love of her life had worsened her. Still, not even on her darkest days, did I ever wish she would lose her life.

She passed away in the early morning on my sixteenth birthday.

THURSDAY AFTERNOON

# Alaina

I arrived at O'Hare Airport in Chicago. The driver from the car service I'd arranged was waiting outside the gate to take me to my hotel. Taxis were disgusting, and I didn't trust those private ride request apps. With a true car service, I knew I would receive quiet and safe transportation in a clean and reliable vehicle. I also knew the driver would not try to make mindless conversation with me, or worse, attempt to flirt with me. I purposely chose the best-rated hotel within walking distance from the art gallery. I did everything in my power to make this trip as easy as possible for myself. In and out. Quick and painless.

*Best laid plans.*

The moment I entered the hotel room and set down my suitcase next to the bed, my phone rang. It was Dex. Dexter Christian and my father were best friends growing up in Chicago. They joined the military together after high school. He was my godfather, in an unofficial, non-religious capacity. Immediately following my mother's death, Dex set his own life aside to make sure I had all the support and guidance I needed. He moved into my family home to help me care for it, and assisted me with the process of graduating high school and entering college two years ahead of schedule. He was my best friend and my only family.

"Hi," I answered. "I just walked into my hotel room." I had insisted he not step away from his work to retrieve me from the airport himself.

"Hey, Lainey. I'm glad you made it okay. How was your flight?"

"It was fine. How are you? How's everything going?"

"I couldn't be better. Everything came together beautifully, come by whenever you're ready. I can't wait for you to see the exhibit."

"I can't wait to see *you*. I'll freshen up and head down shortly."

"Sounds good."

I walked through the doors of Meridian Gallery and was immediately overcome by my mother's energy. Her presence was as tangible as my own.

"Hey there," Dex walked across the gallery floor with his arms outstretched. "I missed you." His hugs we absolutely therapeutic for me.

"I missed you, too."

"Come have a look," he said with a sly smile. "I think you're going to be pleasantly surprised."

I had been dreading this for months, and suddenly I found myself strangely eager. The tapping of my high heels on the hardwood floors echoed through the gallery as I carefully examined every display while tugging at my lips, deep in thought. Dex had done a remarkable job of selecting and acquiring the perfect two-dimensional artwork to pair with every piece of my mother's pottery, and styling each display with simple organic elements like branches, sea glass, and natural stones. I could hear the clear blue waves gently folding into the shoreline, the seagulls calling down from the sky, as I looked at them. I could feel the warmth of the sun and picture the sugar sand beach where she and my father would walk together in her dreams.

Her ceramics had always seemed so dull and lifeless to me in her studio – pale, bland, and bleak. Created for no real purpose than to pass the time as her health declined, and looked upon only until completely cooled, then immediately boxed, bound and gagged by packing materials. Here, they felt entirely different. A visible piece of her soul was embedded within them. They breathed deeply and whispered stories. Their shapes captured the drifts of the sand and the swirls of the waves, the billowing of their clothing in the gentle breeze, and the strands of her long, wavy hair being softly carried by the wind. This is what she had been doing all the while, trying desperately to reconstruct in her reality what she had discovered inside her dreams. Dex understood this. He spent years trying to convince me to let him exhibit her collection, and my resentment for her wouldn't allow me to consider it. I couldn't understand why he would want to do this for her after the way she treated me. I now understood this was never for her. It had always been for me.

"Oh, before I forget, I found this inside one of the crates," he pulled a small, hardcover notebook from his pocket and handed it to me. It had a linen fabric cover – French white, just like her pottery – with a matching ribbon affixed within the binding. "I assume it's another one of your mother's journals. I opened it just to the first page, to see what it was. It's written in French."

All of my mother's personal journals were larger, dark and leather-bound. They were a gift from my father every Christmas, starting with their first. He thought it would be a good way for her to practice her English, but while she did take to journaling religiously throughout her life, she always wrote in French. I couldn't be certain, but perhaps it was a way to hold on to who she was, to remember where she came from no matter where life took her. It was also a possibility that I was just trying to give her a piece of rationale I could relate to.

I obsessively read every one of her journals after she died. I struggled with whether or not it was right to read them, but I wanted so desperately to understand her. Reading her innermost thoughts only increased my pain. They were never meant for me to see, that was clear by the dark and raw things she wrote about. I read them again at eighteen or so, and then again at twenty-two, hoping that my growing self-awareness would afford me a different view of her. Unfortunately, that was not the case, and I decided I would not read them again.

This notebook couldn't be another journal, it had to be something else. I thanked Dex as I tucked it into my purse. This wasn't the time or the place to open it. Everything my mother did was dramatic and self-indulgent, and most often hurtful to me. I was certain that whatever was written inside this notebook was something I'd prefer to read later, when I was alone – if at all.

On the cusp of evening, after making sure everything was perfect for the exhibit's opening reception the following night, Dex locked the gallery doors and we walked back to my hotel to have a nice dinner together at its street-level restaurant. It was much easier to enjoy, being a weekday evening and outside of the most common dining hours. I had made a habit of doing most things in life at the least common times. It kept things simpler, easier to predict.

The moment we were seated, Dex got right down to business. "So, tell me, are you seeing anyone?"

I really wasn't interested in seeing anyone. He knew that. I had always preferred to remain focused on my studies, and later on, my research work. I strived for constant self-improvement, to learn as much as possible in my lifetime, and to hopefully contribute something worthwhile to humanity before I came to the end of it. This, and remaining dedicated to the care of my family home, left me with little time or energy for social interaction. People were exhausting to me. I would much rather live vicariously through art, books, and films. It was cleaner. Easier to remove yourself from when you've had enough. I envied the secondary life my mother had in her dreams. What I wouldn't give for the ability to throw caution to the wind, take chances and live freely, love freely, knowing I could return to a life unaltered by it.

"No, I'm not seeing anyone," I admitted. "I'm between research projects for the remainder of the summer. Now that the guest house isn't full of pottery, I thought I might use this time to renovate it. At the very least, it needs a good cleaning and a fresh coat of paint. The plumbing probably needs some attention, it hasn't been used in eight years.

Simon Kincaid offered me another permanent position with his research group in London, starting this fall. He also mentioned again that he would like to start seeing each other, and suggested that if I were to take him up on both offers, I should move in with him."

Dex picked up his drink and took a swig. "How do you feel about that?"

"Well, as far as the work goes, my consciousness studies would be fully funded by one of the most innovative research groups in the world. I would have consistent meaningful work, a dedicated facility and staff at my disposal, and a first-rate compensation package. I certainly wouldn't miss the long flights back and forth to London every few months.

As far as Simon goes… I know him well. I trust and respect him. He's incredibly smart, and a very gifted scientist. We understand each other. The work is every bit as important to him as it is to me, and we have always worked well together. We do feel like partners in that respect. He understands the level of dedication and the long hours our field demands. From that perspective, residing in the same place would have its conveniences. But being in a relationship with a supervising colleague is rarely a wise idea, nor does it typically end well. I would hate to jeopardize the wonderful relationship we have, just to find out whether we could be more. Besides, I enjoy being alone. I'm good at it. I know what to expect from myself."

"I didn't hear a single word in there that sounded like attraction, and that's perfectly fine. Simon would clearly be a safe choice, which is all I've ever seen you make. The last thing in the world I want is for you to get hurt or lose ground, but I also don't want you to go through life without ever taking a real chance on someone, without ever knowing what it's like to fall in love, get your heart broken, bounce back, and do it all again.

I know I'm not your father, Lainey, but please let me give you one piece of fatherly advice... If you truly want to devote your life to researching the mysteries of human consciousness and behavior, then you need to get out there and stick your damn foot in it. Think of it as a field study."

*I didn't own a single pair of shoes I was willing to do that in.*

"First, please don't ever say you're not my father. You are every bit as much of a father to me as my father was. Second, I do understand your point. It's just that... The New York house is the only place that feels like home to me. You're the only person who feels like home to me. I've never taken a permanent position anywhere because I find comfort in returning to my family home between work assignments, just as my father had. It's more than just returning home, it's returning to myself. I'm very familiar with London. I love it there. I'm comfortable there. But it's never felt like home to me, and neither has Simon."

Dex downed the last of his drink just as the bill arrived. He placed his hand on top of the black faux leather check presenter and slid it over to his side of the table before pulling out his wallet.

"Fair enough. Just keep in mind that feelings can, and do, change. Look what happened when you finally opened the tomb of your mother's work and allowed it to exist in the world, beyond the confines of her studio. You learned more about who she was and what she was experiencing than you ever could by reading her journals. You gave her a chance to exist beyond who you knew her to be. That may have seemed like a solitary choice on your part, but it will change the course of things for more than just you and me. This work is her life story, and this exhibit will teach people about themselves. It will move and inspire them. That's the magic of art, Alaina, of human creation.

Look… Your family home isn't going anywhere. I'm not going anywhere. Your work isn't going anywhere. You could go home and renovate the guest house, or you could use this transitional time to do something that scares the hell out of you. Let it move and inspire you, let it change the course of things, and let it change your life."

"Honor the space between no longer
and not yet." —Nancy Levin

## THURSDAY NIGHT

*Alaina*

I returned to my hotel room and locked the door behind me. After spending some time checking emails and returning texts, I closed the curtains, completed my nightly routine, and climbed into bed. I carefully thought about Dexter's words to me. *Did my course need to change?* This certainly was a transitional time in my life, and perhaps I was standing at the threshold of a life-altering opportunity. I hated to think that by striving to make the very best use of my life, I had been failing to actually live it. That was never my intent.

My mind drifted to the concept of liminality, derived from the Latin word limen, meaning threshold. Liminal time was the term used to define the transitory moment between when part of life is ending and another is beginning, where the landscape is foreign and the outcome is uncertain. The term liminal space identified a transitory location, a waystation of sorts, that was used temporarily to get from one place to another.

The concept of liminality suggested that where liminal time and liminal space intersected – outside the limitations of what was considered to be normal – the extraordinary became possible, the inexplicable often occurred, and the metaphysical could sometimes be experienced. While many people had reported encountering this intersection accidentally, no one to my knowledge had determined how to arrive there deliberately.

This was my last memory.

"The person you never saw coming
will be the one to change your life."
—Unknown

# FRIDAY MORNING

## Jake

From an architectural standpoint, I had an appreciation for this godawful house. I admired its quality craftsmanship and intricate detail every time I rushed to get the hell out of it. It was dark and heavy. Oppressive. Full of strangely moving shadows, even during the day. Maybe it wasn't the house at all, but everything that had happened here over time, that accounted for its unsettling atmosphere. It had a long and sordid history filled with greed, cruelty, and torment. I hated coming here as a kid, and I hated living here now – if you could call what I was doing living. It was a place to crash between work shifts, and that was about it. It had never felt like home to me, and I doubted it ever would.

Caris kept the whole place on lockdown. She looked out the windows often, but she never opened them. We'd been breathing the exact same stale air for the last eight years. This house hadn't seen a gathering, or a guest, since her mother was taken away many years ago. I'd given up on the idea of ever having a family of my own. It was way too much house for just the two of us, but Caris found ways to reasonably maintain it without hiring outside help. She never let anyone but the two of us inside the gates, aside from deliveries. I suggested many times that we look for something smaller and newer, closer to the hospital, and less isolated. Less doom and gloom, was what I really wanted to say. Many of my colleagues and friends had places along the more habitable part of the lakefront, within walking distance from the hospital, among other things. Things we never did. Caris wouldn't hear of it. She insisted we remain in this unapproachable manor, seated high up on the cliffs in the center of several other unapproachable manors, along one of the most treacherous parts of the lake. Even though she'd never even tried living anywhere else, she was convinced that this was the only place that would ever feel like home to her. She didn't really seem concerned with what would feel like home to me.

"Why don't you just order it online and have it shipped directly to her house?" Caris followed me down the main staircase, through the first floor rooms, and into the kitchen. Every minute I spent inside this house, she was either right next to me, coming toward me, or following me. I seldom had a moment to myself. She typically slept during the day, and would have taken her pills and gone to bed by now, but on my days off she tried to keep herself awake as long as she could.

"I enjoy going to the bookstore, and besides, I think it makes a gift more mean-ingful when you make the time and effort to purchase and deliver it personal-ly." I stopped myself from verbalizing the many other thoughts I was having at that moment, thoughts along the lines of, God forbid I should do something as normal as buy my mom a book for her birthday. It was frustrating to have to explain and justify something so simple. I made sure I had my phone, wallet, and keys on me. As long as I had those three things, I could handle any situa-tion life decided to throw at me that day.

"I could go with you."

I knew where she was going with this. She thought I was meeting a woman. I was not, nor had I ever been, in love with my wife. She was well aware of that. But I did care about her, and I made a commitment to her. I made a promise to her father, and to mine. Even as lonely and unhappy as I was after eight years in this bizarre marriage, I had never cheated on my wife. Had I thought about it? Of course. What man in my position wouldn't? But I had never acted on those thoughts, and I never would. I was in this marriage because I have always done what was best for everyone else, done what was expected of me, contrary to my own wants and needs. My purpose in this life was to help others, and it was a noble one. I could live with that. A man without integrity was not a man.

"I'd really like to take my motorcycle, Caris. I barely get a chance to ride it. You hate the bike." I bought this old Harley when I turned eighteen. It felt like a piece of freedom, especially now that freedom had become so evasive to me.

"It's going to rain," she said under her breath, arms crossed and looking away from me, annoyed. She had a childlike way about her at times.

I looked out the kitchen window, overlooking the patio where the pool used to be. There wasn't a cloud in the sky. I gave her a quick obligatory kiss on the cheek. "Don't forget to take your pills. I'll be back before you know it."

The best bookstore in Chicago was right next door to the coffeehouse with the best Americanos. There were two types of people in this world. Those who drank real coffee, and those who drank sugar milk with a hint of coffee flavor. It was one of my favorite places to go on my days off, but I didn't get there very often. I liked taking the motorcycle on good weather days, not to mention it was much easier to park on the city streets. It was my lucky day. A cab pulled away just as I rolled up to the front entrance of the bookstore, and I was able to slide right into the open spot.

Coffee before books.

The morning rush was over and I was able to step right up to the counter. Again, my lucky day. I placed my order and stepped off to the side to wait for it, checking my phone. It was a relief, as well as a surprise, that I didn't already have a text or a missed call from Caris.

"Americano for Jake?" the barista shouted.

I grabbed my to-go cup at the pick-up end of the counter and headed for the bookstore. I immediately located the book my mom wanted for her birthday, it was displayed among the staff picks at the front of the store. *The Midnight Library*. I found a nature book that interested me and sat down to look through it while I drank my coffee. It felt good to be alone, and anywhere other than the house or the hospital. Most days, life was just going to work, and going back home. I got lost in the book I was reading, finally looking up when I realized I was taking a sip from an empty cup. I glanced out the bookstore windows and noticed the sky had grown dark. Caris was right, there was a storm coming. I would have liked to stay longer, but I figured I should try to get ahead of the weather. It was miserable, not to mention unsafe, to ride a motorcycle in the rain.

I spotted a few small raindrops on the black leather sleeve of my motorcycle jacket as I placed my mom's book into the side compartment of the bike. When I stood up to reach for my helmet, I saw a beautiful woman crossing the intersection, headed in my direction. Man, she was something. Have you ever seen someone who was just…bright? A literal light in the world. She looked so familiar to me, but if we'd met before there was no way I'd forget it. I glanced down for just a second, fidgeting with the temperamental retention strap on my helmet before putting it on.

It happened so quickly.

A deep, sickening thud pierced the air and echoed through the entire intersection. A bedlam of screeching tires and shrieking voices ensued. The beautiful woman was lying in the street. Without thinking, I instantly jumped over the front of the bike and rushed into the crosswalk to help her.

I fought my way through the crowd quickly forming around her and bent down next to her. She was unconscious. Unresponsive. I picked up her hand to check for a pulse and felt something strange, like an electrical current, that passed from her hand into mine. It traveled up my arm and circulated throughout my entire body. Time stood still for a moment, and everything going on around me suddenly quieted. I'd never been in physical contact with someone as they died before, but I sure hoped this wasn't what it felt like.

"Stay with me," I said softly to her as I set down her hand so I could grab my phone from my back pocket and call 9-1-1. "I need an ambulance on the corner of Michigan and Third, please. A woman has been hit by a car."

Pulse located. I checked for any airway obstructions. Clear. I watched her chest and abdomen for movement. I listened for breath sounds and felt for airflow. She was breathing on her own, thank God. I assessed her surface injuries. No apparent broken bones. No severe external bleeding. Surface scrapes to the hands and face, likely from hitting the pavement. Notable head contusion. Possible concussion.

The distant sound of the ambulance siren grew louder as it drew closer to the accident scene. I removed my motorcycle jacket, rolled it into a makeshift pillow, and carefully placed it under her head. There was nothing else I could do for her on the street without any equipment. I looked upward and scanned the area around me, searching for anyone else who might need medical attention. No one else appeared to have been hit. "Is the driver injured?" I called out. "Is there anyone else in the vehicle?"

People looked back and forth at one another, but nobody said a word. Finally, a woman toward the front of the crowd apologetically offered me a response. "The vehicle never stopped." *Are you kidding me? Who would do that?* Hit and runs unfortunately weren't a rarity, for any major city. Still, it never ceased to amaze me just how someone could knowingly harm another human being and not take responsibility for their actions.

The ambulance weaved its way through traffic to us, just as it began to pour. The crowd scattered to get out of the rain, and out of the way, as the paramedics rushed forward carrying their equipment and a stretcher. They were acquaintances from the hospital's employee fitness center and the occasional pickup basketball game behind the hospital between shifts.

"Jake, what have we got?"

"Hit and run while crossing the street. She's unconscious but stable, slight head injury, possible concussion. No other obvious issues. She'll need to be evaluated for internal injuries and neurological trauma."

"Did she ever get lucky. Anyone else hurt?"

"No. Somehow it was only her."

"We've got her from here." They lifted her onto the stretcher.

Still kneeling on the ground, I watched as they loaded the woman into the back of the ambulance, closed the doors, and pulled away. A doorman from a nearby building had been re-routing traffic down a side street until the scene cleared. Everything simply began again, just as quickly as it had come to a halt, as if nothing out of the ordinary had happened at all. Normal traffic resumed, and I was suddenly being honked at to get out of the street. *Nice.* I grabbed my jacket off the ground to find her purse lying underneath it. I picked it up and jogged back to the sidewalk outside the bookstore.

I took it slow getting the bike home in the rain.

"In yourself right now is all the place you've got."
—Flannery O'Connor

FRIDAY NIGHT

## Jake

I lay awake in bed, staring through the open bathroom door at my water-damaged leather jacket hanging over the glass shower door, going over every single detail of the incident in my mind. I kept telling myself that there was nothing more I could have done for her. I followed protocol and did everything by the book. The hospital would notify the police, if the paramedics hadn't already. Unfortunately, I didn't see anything that could help them determine who did this. She wasn't my patient, and I didn't know her.

*But I wanted to.*

I wanted to learn everything I could about her. I felt so guilty for wanting that, for being so intrigued by her and feeling so drawn to her, but I couldn't help it. It wasn't about her beauty, although she was certainly a stunner. It was about needing to understand what it was I felt when I first saw her, when I touched her hand in the street, and desperately wanting to feel it again. There was a warmth and light that radiated from her, something pure and ethereal that made her seem otherworldly, like an angel that had fallen to the earth. Even unconscious and injured, she was somehow more of a comfort to me than I could be to her. I had no other way to describe it than she felt like home. Now that I knew she existed in this world, I had to know her. I had to be part of her life.

I wanted so badly to open her purse – which was now hidden in the awkward space behind the drawer of my nightstand – just so I could fall asleep knowing her name, but it would have been dishonorable to open it. It was bothering me enough that I still had it with me. I could have, and maybe should have, brought it to the hospital that afternoon, but I couldn't bring myself to part with it just yet. I knew how creepy that sounded, and I wasn't comfortable with how that made me feel about myself. I also recognized that this was the first time I'd ever deliberately hidden something from my wife, and I wasn't comfortable with how that made me feel either.

I didn't need to know her name tonight when I could learn it tomorrow without invading her privacy. Relying on my moral compass to steer me away from what I wanted was something I'd become incredibly skilled at. If I was meant to know her, then I needed to make certain I remained a man worth knowing, and let fate do its job.

I decided it was best to head to the hospital first thing in the morning and check on her before my shift, as the doctor who helped her on the scene. That was fair. There was a strong chance she'd be awake by then. I could introduce myself, return her purse, and speak to her directly.

*Best laid plans.*

# FRIDAY NIGHT

## Alaina

I regained consciousness within an unresponsive body.

I was surrounded by nothing but complete darkness. Stillness. Nothingness. I could tell my eyes were closed and I was lying down. I was chilled to the bone. The last thing I remembered was going to sleep in my hotel room. I could picture the room around me in my mind's eye, but I had no way to know if I was picturing the truth.

*What was happening to me?*

Fear flowed through every inch of my body, like ice-cold water rushing through a lifting floodgate. I couldn't move. I couldn't speak. I was held in place by some kind of invisible force, alone in a way I had never been before.

Sleep paralysis seemed unlikely. Though I was experiencing many of its symptoms, sleep paralysis only lasted from a few seconds to a few minutes. This felt much longer, though I couldn't be certain. Time felt somehow suspended, like in a dream state.

*Was I dead?*

I had always wondered if there was truly life after death, or if the end was simply the end. What if there was something in between the two? Not between heaven and hell, or between religion and atheism, but a consciousness between life and death itself.

Theories on the nature of human consciousness differed greatly around the world, between varying cultures, philosophies, and religions. Science declared all living things to be conscious beings inhabiting bodies of matter. Matter, as we have come to understand it, must obey the laws of physics. Consciousness, on the other hand, may transcend those laws. While matter relies on consciousness, consciousness does not rely on matter. Your standard one-sided relationship. I knew a lot about those as well.

A soul is bestowed upon the birth of every human life, and severed upon its death. Many people resonate with the belief that the soul is infinite, and will experience several human lifetimes as a means of evolution through trial. Pierre Teilhard de Chardin was credited with the concept that within each of us lies an innate knowledge of our infinite spiritual nature, but the tribulations of human existence cause us to lose sight of who we are and what we know at a soul level. He was also of the belief that not all souls are inherently good.

Death was not a possibility either. I had an unsettling awareness of my heart beating, like an echoing metronome relentlessly keeping time within my cavernous hull. Even a quiet sound can be deafening when it's the only sound you hear.

I read a short story once, about a woman who had been buried alive. She regained consciousness within her coffin, buried underground. She, too, was surrounded by complete darkness. Stillness. Nothingness. She panicked, cried, and screamed. She kicked, scraped, and pushed. She inhaled the metallic scent of her own blood as she wiped her tears away with wounded hands, and accepted her fate. She quickly transitioned from fighting for her life, to impatiently waiting for her last breath to be drawn. Would it be this one? Would it be the next? Until eventually, her heart stopped beating.

Among the many things that always bothered me about this story were, who was telling it, how were they telling it, and to whom? It certainly suggested that her consciousness survived her death, and furthermore, found a way to successfully communicate with the living.

Could you imagine, if this were the truth of life after death? No divine splendor, no fiery damnation, just our own consciousness, echoing and persistent, existing without the burden of being bound to matter. What I wouldn't give to prove, or even disprove, that theory.

I felt my consciousness fade away.

"A single dream is more powerful than a thousand realities."
—Nathaniel Hawthorne

SATURDAY MORNING

*Jake*

I barely slept. The events of the day before replayed in my mind every time I managed to fall asleep, each version a little bit further from the truth. In the first dream, I stood next to my motorcycle while scanning the crowd for her, but she wasn't there at all. In the next, our eyes met as she began crossing the intersection, just as they actually had, but then she disappeared behind a passing car before reaching the other side. In yet another, I never saw her crossing the street at all. I was looking down at the bike when I heard a voice say, "Hello, Jake." I looked up to find her standing right in front of me, so close that I could smell her perfume and see her blue-gray eyes sparkle in the sunlight. In reality, I hadn't had the good fortune to look into her eyes or hear her say my name.

I left the house much earlier than usual, while Caris was still out for her run, and arrived at the hospital before sunrise. The overnight skeleton crew was still on duty, and after-hours protocols were still in effect. I logged into the nearest computer to find out her room number and take a look at her case file. She was stable, but had not yet regained consciousness, and was still classified as a Jane Doe. *That was on me.* Her CT scan determined she had no internal injuries, bleeding, or organ damage. A full set of X-rays confirmed no broken bones, fractures, or dislocations. All labs came back clean. She did indeed get very lucky.

I grabbed a cup of coffee and headed for the bank of elevators that would take me to the long-term care floor. My muscles tensed and my heart pounded as I moved through the quiet hospital toward her room. This moment was all I'd thought about since I watched as the ambulance took her away from me. The moment I would see her again. I wondered what she would be like, and if she would be as drawn to me as I was to her. I wanted her to be. I wanted that flow of energy to occur again, and I wanted her to feel it, too.

If a person's presence could speak of who they are, then I was certain she was genuine, caring, and kind. She was surely smart and well-spoken, and if my dream was any indication, she had the soothing voice of an angel. But I longed to know the true details of her – the things I didn't dare assume. The things and people that mattered the most to her in this world, and how she expressed her love for them. The music she listened to, and if she was the kind of person to stay in the car until the song she loved ended. The books she read, and if she was the type to stick with a story just to see how it ended. If she was the type to read the books she loved over and over again. I knew I had already dangerously built her up to be the person I'd been dreaming of all my life. My soulmate. The one and only person who could relieve the emptiness I felt deep within my heart. The one I was meant to give my everything to. A hopeless thought, since no matter how amazing she was and what might exist between us, I was not available to be with her. For all I knew, she was unavailable as well.

Upon learning that she was still unconscious, my thoughts shifted to an embarrassing and unrealistic fairytale hope that sensing me there would be all it took to revive her. I desperately wanted to be all she needed. I paused for a moment and took a deep breath before opening the door to her hospital room. I closed the door behind me and left the lights turned off, so I wouldn't draw attention to my being there. I sat down in the chair next to her bed in the quiet room, setting the cup of terrible hospital coffee on the bedside table. I wasn't going to drink it. Nobody should. I'd read somewhere that a surprising number of coma patients physically responded to the smell of strong coffee, and that most who reawakened did so right around sunrise. I figured both were worth a shot.

"Good morning," I said softly. "Would you like to watch the sunrise together?" I smiled when I spoke to her, though I knew she couldn't see it. Once when I was a kid, I asked my mom why she always smiled when she talked on the phone. She said it was because you could hear a smile in someone's voice. I never forgot that. "My name is Jake Matthews. I was nearby when you were hurt yesterday. You're in the hospital, and I'm a doctor here. I want you to know that you're going to be just fine. I reviewed your case file this morning, and everything looks great. I'm not sure why you haven't woken up yet, but I'm going to figure that out and do everything I can to help you, I promise. You can count on me."

The rising sun streamed in from the window behind me, creating a glowing aura around her in the otherwise dark room. She squinted. It was barely there, but I knew I saw it. I leaned in and touched her cheek with the back of my hand. Energy once again flowed from her, into and through me. I was relieved to experience it again. Her head turned into my hand, ever so slightly, confirming to me that she felt it as well. We connected somehow. I couldn't explain it, but I knew it. I brushed her hair away from her face and pleaded with her to open her eyes.

The overnight nurse came into the room to check her vitals one last time before the shift change. We startled each other. "Oh! Good morning, Dr. Matthews. I'm so sorry to interrupt you. I didn't realize this was your patient."

"Good morning, Maggie," I stood up and moved toward the end of the bed so she had room to do her job. "Actually, she's not. I happened to be in the square yesterday when she was struck. I called the ambulance and completed the initial diagnostics on the scene. I just wanted to see how she was doing this morning."

"Oh my goodness, how lucky for her that you were there. She's doing quite well, all things considered. Her injuries are surprisingly minimal. The police have asked to be notified as soon as she regains consciousness. Until then, they were going to look for possible security footage in the area."

The automatic lights switched to the daylight setting and the hallway became more active. The overnight shift had ended, which meant mine had just begun. "I hope they're able to figure out who did this. I better get to work. If her primary doctor requests a neurological consult, I'd like it to be me."

"Yes, of course. I will make that note in the case file before I head home."

"Thanks, Maggie. Have a good day."

"You too, Dr. Matthews."

## SATURDAY NIGHT

### Jake

Hospital weekends were notoriously chaotic and under-staffed in the summer. Most doctors didn't want to work weekends if they could avoid it, especially this time of year. They preferred to spend that time with their families. My parents were retired, and without any grandchildren to dote on, they spent almost all of their time traveling. My brother was usually on the road somewhere with the sports team he worked with. I caught hell at home anytime I tried to see my friends, so after a while, I just stopped pushing the issue. Weekends were a reminder of the life I didn't have, so I was content to work as much as possible, especially when I could cover a shift in a different part of the hospital and learn something new. I enjoyed helping people, it was a good use of my time, and working in a hospital was always a good reminder that my day could be worse.

That day, all I wanted was the chance to get back to her, but I was lucky just to get a quick bathroom break and thirty seconds to inhale a protein bar. Every time I finished putting out one fire, there was another one waiting for me. It unfortunately wasn't a possibility at this point. If I left right then, I would get home just in time to shower, go to bed, and do it all over again the next day. My phone buzzed in my pocket. I knew it would be Caris, awake and wondering when I was coming home.

"If they're going to insist you work on the weekends, the least they could do is not keep you past your scheduled shift." Caris appeared out of thin air, standing outside the shower. She looked unfamiliar to me, her face distorted and blurred by the fogged glass of the shower wall. The already humid air in the room seemingly thickened with her presence.

"You know how unpredictable the days can be," I answered, talking over the sound of the running water.

"If you and your brother had taken over the private practice like you were supposed to, you could be making your own hours right now."

"Derek is really happy in sports medicine, he loves traveling with the teams. I would never ask him to give that up." I turned off the water and stepped out of the shower, grabbing a towel. "I like being at the hospital, for now, working with other people. I'm alone in every other part of my life, I don't want to work alone, too." I regretted those words the moment they left my mouth and took up residence in the space between us.

"You're not alone, you have me," she replied. "Maybe you should just quit, we don't need the money. Then we could spend all of our time together."

"It's not about the money for me, you know that. I need my life to have a purpose."

"Your purpose is to be with me. Come downstairs and watch a movie with me."

"I can't, Caris. I'm sorry," I hung up the towel and threw on a clean pair of boxers. "I'm due back at the hospital first thing in the morning. You go ahead, I need to get to bed."

The best bookstore in Chicago was right next door to the coffeehouse with the best Americanos. There were two types of people in this world. Those who drank real coffee, and those who drank sugar milk with a hint of coffee flavor. It was one of my favorite places to go on my days off, but I didn't get there very often. I liked taking the motorcycle on good weather days, not to mention it was much easier to park on the city streets. It was my lucky day. A cab pulled away just as I rolled up to the front entrance of the bookstore, and I was able to slide right in.

Books before coffee.

I immediately located the book my mom wanted for her birthday, it was displayed among the staff picks at the front of the store. *The Midnight Library*. I found a nature book that interested me and sat down to look through it. It was a nice way to spend a little time away from the house. Most days, life was just going to work, and going back home.

I exited the bookstore, turning to enter the adjoining coffeehouse, when I collided with a beautiful woman heading in the opposite direction, knocking her down. Her coffee slipped from her hand and fell to the ground, splashing up onto my jeans.

"I'm so sorry," I extended my hand to help her up. "Are you okay?"

"I'm fine," she replied, accepting my hand. I felt something strange, like an electrical current, that passed from her hand into mine. It traveled up my arm and circulated throughout my body. I'd never experienced anything like it before, and the look on her face told me she felt it, too. Once she was on her feet again, she looked at me and smiled, her hand still in mine. Man, she was something. Have you ever seen someone who was just…bright? A literal light in the world. She looked so familiar to me, but if we'd met before there was no way I'd forget it.

"Please, let me replace that for you," we both looked over at her empty, broken coffee cup lying on the ground and laughed a little. "Are you sure you're okay?"

"Yes, I'm fine. Thank you. That really isn't necessary."

"Please. It's the least I can do," I smiled.

She accepted, and waited at a nearby table next to the window, looking out at the busy intersection. I delivered her caramel macchiato to the table, along with an Americano for myself, and asked permission to sit down with her.

"Jake Matthews," I reached across the table to shake her hand, hoping that strange feeling would happen again.

"Alaina Ryan," she smiled, shaking my hand. "I hope your book wasn't damaged. What are you reading?"

"No, I think it's fine. *The Midnight Library*. It's actually a birthday gift for my mom."

"It's such a wonderful book. One of my favorites. I hope she loves it."

I couldn't get enough of the sound of her voice. "What's it about?" I asked, wanting to hear her speak to me at length, about the book, or about anything at all. She could recite the periodic table of elements to me, and I'd be captivated by it.

"It's about a woman who is disappointed with her life. She finds herself in the library between life and death, where she has the opportunity to experience alternate versions of her life. There's much more to it than that, so much layered meaning, but that's the general idea."

"That sounds really interesting. I'll have to pick it up sometime."

"What do you usually enjoy reading?"

"Most of what I read now is work-related. Research and reference. I used to read a lot of Stephen King and Neil Gaiman, when I had the time."

"What sort of work do you do?"

"I'm a doctor at Northwestern. Neurology. What about you?"

"What a small world. I work in neuroscience and quantum physics. I gave a lecture there about a month ago, on the nature of human consciousness. That must be why you look so familiar to me."

"Alaina Ryan, of course. I've read a lot of your research. I really wanted to attend that lecture, but unfortunately, I had to miss it. Something came up at the last minute. Speaking of last minute, is there any chance you're free for dinner tonight? There's so much I'd love to talk to you about."

"I have an art reception to attend in the early evening, but I have some time afterward. Do you like art, would you care to join me?"

"I don't know much about art, but I do like it. That sounds great. I'd love that."

She reached into her purse, pulled out an invitation, and placed it on the table in front of me. "I will meet you there. I have to be going now, but the information is all right here."

"I'll be there."

"Then I look forward to seeing you tonight. It was nice to meet you, Jake. Thank you again for the coffee," she smiled.

"You too. Have a good day," I smiled, standing as she left the table. I watched out the coffeehouse window as she safely crossed the street.

I couldn't wait to meet my brother, Derek, for lunch and tell him I had not only just met Alaina Ryan, but asked her to dinner, and she said yes.

"No fucking way. Are you sure it was really her?"

"Of course I'm sure it was really her."

"Jake…You're a Chicago eight, which makes you what, like a global six? Alaina Ryan is a ten. A global ten. The only way you picked up Alaina Ryan today is if you knocked her down first."

"Well, it's funny you should say that, because that's exactly what happened."

He laughed. "There it is. Did she suffer a head injury? That might explain her momentary lapse in judgment."

"Thanks, D. I appreciate that."

"When's the last time you were even on a date?"

"It's been a while. I don't know, the older I get, the more dating seems like a waste of my time. It's always the same. You text a few times, you get to know the basics…how old are you, what do you do for a living…then comes dinner, where you discover she has an obnoxious laugh, or a childish sense of humor, or she's incapable of an intelligent, meaningful conversation. You convince yourself to give her a second chance, maybe even a third, because sometimes people are awkward and uncomfortable on first dates. Then you realize you were wrong, those awful dates were actually her best foot forward and it's all going downhill from here, so you cut your losses and get to know the next one. It starts to feel like self-inflicted torture after a while, don't you think?"

"I wouldn't know. I skip the torture and get right to the good part. There's no shortage of women willing to sleep with you, Jake. I've seen the way women look at you. Just hook up when you feel like it, and get everything else you need from your family and friends. That's what I do."

"I'm not like you. Sometimes I wish I could be. I want to find my soulmate. I want the kind of love Mom and Dad have. I want a family of my own, with someone who will never get tired of me and sleep with someone else."

"It's been eight years, Jake, you've got to let that go. Caris did you a favor, man. You were forced on each other, it never would've worked out. Most marriages don't. Not everybody is like Mom and Dad, and that Hallmark movie happiness doesn't actually exist. Look at our friends who got married, almost all of them are miserable. The ones who think they're happy don't even realize how flabby and boring they are now. Be glad you and Caris never made it down the aisle. If you really want to experience unconditional love, just adopt a dog. At least we can take it hiking."

"Good evening, sir. May I have your name and invitation, please?"

"Jake Matthews," I handed him the invitation Alaina had given me at the coffeehouse.

"Dr. Matthews," he placed a check mark on the last page of his list, took the invitation, and handed me a small card in exchange. "If you'd care for drinks, just show this card at the bar. Right through here. Enjoy your evening, sir."

"Thank you."

I slowly walked around the gallery, following the flow of foot traffic, casually looking for Alaina as I took in the exhibit. I spotted her toward the back of the gallery, speaking to someone. She looked beautiful in her dark blue dress and heels, her long hair flowing down in soft curls. She smiled when she noticed me. Now that she knew I was there, I continued circulating until she had the chance to break away.

I heard her soft, elegant voice behind me, "I'm so glad you could make it. I'm sorry to have kept you waiting. Are you enjoying the exhibit?"

"I am, very much," I smiled. "I've never seen artwork paired like this, with pottery. It's amazing."

"Alaina, who's your friend?" We turned to face the imposing older gentleman standing behind us. He had short black hair, dark skin, and black ink tattoos peeking out from the edges of his collar and sleeves.

"Jake, this is Dexter Christian. Dex, this is Jake Matthews." We shook hands and exchanged greetings. "This is my mother's pottery," she went on. "They've been packed away in her studio since she passed away. Dex finally talked me into allowing him to build an exhibit around them."

"And I was right, as I tend to be," he teased. He looked past us, toward the entrance. "It looks like I'm being summoned," he shook my hand a second time. "It was a pleasure to meet you, sir."

"You too," I smiled. We continued to walk through the exhibit. "How do you two know each other?"

"Dex is my godfather. My father was killed in action when I was twelve. My mother became ill shortly after that, and she passed away when I was sixteen. Dex stepped in and became my family."

"I'm sorry you lost your parents at such a young age. That had to be hard. Not that it isn't hard at any age."

"Thank you," she gracefully adjusted the subject. "What's your family like?"

"My parents are really great. My dad is a doctor, and my mother was a nurse before they got married. I have one brother, Derek. He's in sports medicine – a team doctor, so he travels a lot, but we're still very close. We still have the same group of friends we grew up with, give or take a few. I take it you didn't grow up here?"

"No. We traveled here twice I believe, when I was very small. Once to visit my grandfather, and once more for his funeral. I don't remember either trip. My father mainly worked in Europe. He met my mother while on leave in the French Mediterranean, where she was from. It was love at first sight. They eloped immediately, and a year later I was born."

"Please don't tell me you still live in Europe."

"No," she smiled. "I live in New York. My father inherited a beautiful country estate in Pound Ridge. It had been in his mother's family for generations, and belongs to me now. We traveled until I was of school age, then my father wanted me to have a real home and a quality education. It was mainly just my mother and I, he was away on assignment most of the time. It's the only place in the world that has ever really felt like home to me."

"I can understand that. I have a loft in the city close to the hospital, but it's mainly just a place to shower and sleep between hospital shifts. The house I grew up in will always be home to me." I pulled my phone from my pocket to check the time. "I made a dinner reservation for 7:00, will that be okay?"

"Yes, of course," she glanced over the crowded gallery floor. "Let me just find Dexter and say goodbye."

I took her to my favorite Italian place on Navy Pier, where we discussed a wide range of topics like neuroscience, art, philosophy, religion, spirituality, architecture, and astronomy. She was intelligent, thoughtful, and inspiring. I hoped she thought the same of me.

Exiting the restaurant, I looked over my shoulder at the ferry boat docked behind us. "What would you say to a boat ride? I know it's a little touristy, but there's no better view of the city at night."

"Honestly, I would love that. I never really get to experience the city when I'm here."

It was a beautiful, clear night and the water was calm. The boat was fairly empty and quiet, on its final run of the night. I pointed out several buildings of significance and told her what I knew about them, as we stood along the starboard railing. When I ran out of buildings, I began showing her the constellations.

"I'm surprised you can see so many stars in the middle of the city," she said. "Plato believed that every soul has a companion star it returns to after death. I always thought that was such a lovely idea."

The ferry wobbled for a moment as it turned inward, back toward the dock. I instinctively put my arms around her to keep her safe, warm, and steady. She wasn't exactly dressed to be on a clunky old ferry boat. With her permission, I leaned in and lightly touched my lips to hers. Holding her in my arms and kissing her was a thousand times more powerful than the energy that had passed through our hands when we first met. I didn't know what I was feeling, only that I wanted to feel it for the rest of my life.

"Am I ever going to see you again? This can't be it."

"This isn't it," she whispered.

I woke from the dream, still able to feel her lips against mine, the energy that flowed between us still coursing through my body. It felt so real to me that my mind nearly overwrote the truth.

I looked around the dark bedroom, disappointed to realize where I was. Caris wasn't in the window seat tonight. I leaned over and turned on the bedside lamp, retrieving the purse from its hiding place behind my nightstand drawer. I had to open it. I honestly hated to do that, but this was no longer a matter of curiosity. I had to know immediately if she'd really just identified herself to me in a dream. If not, I had one hell of an imagination.

I took a deep breath and carefully popped open the magnetic metal closure on the front of her small leather purse. It was modest and organized inside. Her phone was in a matching leather case. Unsurprisingly, it was dead, and I didn't have the right type of cord to charge it. I took out her wallet, also matching, and opened the flap. There was her driver's license, front and center. I paused to gaze at her photo for a moment. Even in a driver's license photo, she was beautiful. Alaina M. Ryan. Pound Ridge, New York. I couldn't believe it. It made sense that I would know her scent and the feel of her skin, I'd taken note of those things in the street. But her name, where she lived... Those were things I could not know. There was also a small white notebook inside, which I hoped would hold some useful information, but it was written in French. She mentioned in the dream that her mother was from the Mediterranean. Another validation. With those three items removed, I noticed a postcard clinging to the back wall of her purse and slid it out. It was the invitation to the art reception we attended together in my dream. Meridian Gallery. Chicago, Illinois. The same gallery where Caris occasionally assisted.

She was communicating with me. I didn't understand how it was possible, but I knew for certain that she was.

"Happiness resides not in possessions, and not in gold, happiness dwells in the soul." —Democritus

# SATURDAY NIGHT

## *Caris*

I sat alone in the dark watching countless Netflix previews, unable to decide on something to watch. I was too distracted. Too upset. How could he say that to me? How dare he say he's always alone? I went out of my way to be available to him every waking minute that he was at home, which wasn't nearly often enough. He was always too busy or too tired for me.

This house had everything. A greenhouse, a tennis court, a library, a game room, a home theater, a gym… Anything we didn't already have, we had the means to obtain. We could even put back the pool if he wanted to. My father saw to it there was little to need or want beyond these gates. The house was always neat, clean, and quiet. That wouldn't be the case with a house full of children. Suppose we had children, where would he be? Always working no doubt, leaving me to be a married single mother.

Jake could stand to show a little more appreciation for everything he gained by marrying me. He had no idea the things I'd done, and would continue to do, to keep him. I would sooner burn that hospital to the ground than allow it to stand between us. He belonged to me.

"Love is composed of a single soul inhabiting two bodies." —Aristotle

SATURDAY NIGHT

*Alaina*

My consciousness returned to my body. I knew I must have traveled some-where, but I had no memory of it. I was once again confined within myself, only this time, I was able to pick up on the external sound of my breathing. I had to be in a coma. It was the only remaining explanation. *But why?*

After my father's death, my mother was asleep more often than she was awake. At first, I assumed it was the complete exhaustion that accompanied her de-pression and grief. Once we learned she was also gravely ill, I had something else to blame. To an extent, both played a part, but there was a piece of the truth missing. The day she confided in me that while she was asleep, she was able to spend time with my father in her dreams, it finally made sense to me. In her dream world, in this alternate reality she was somehow able to visit, he wasn't dead. He had returned home safely. They spent their days together maintaining the house and gardens, taking walks on the beach, sharing beauti-ful meals, and making love. Part of me was so happy that she'd found a way to be with him that brought her some peace, whether or not it was real to anyone but her. Another part of me was crushed to know that in her dream world, I ceased to exist. She had written me out of their story.

It was what she experienced that led me to my life's work of studying the realms of human consciousness and the possibility of alternate realities. I wanted to understand it. To understand her. I prayed countless times to receive a dream where I could see my father again, but I never dreamed. If I did, I had no memory of it. In my sleep, I often received something else. I awoke with new knowledge; guidance, from somewhere outside of myself. It was impossible to know its exact source, or whether the information was reliable, but it often led me to advances in my work.

Several scientific studies, including some of my own, investigated the possibility that dreams could provide glimpses into parallel dimensions. These dimensions were thought to exist simultaneously alongside our reality, yet remain hidden to our waking consciousness. Perhaps in some other place and time, my father's fate had been different. Somewhere he was alive and well, but all alone, and desperate to meet in his reality the woman who often graced his dreams. Maybe there was an emptiness in him that he couldn't quite explain because some part of him knew what he cherished in another life.

I felt my consciousness fade once again.

A MONTH AGO

## Caris

It was my first opportunity to handle an evening delivery and pre-installation at Meridian Gallery. Dexter Christian, the owner and curator, worked tirelessly to create this exhibit and acquire the works. He had a rare talent for concepting and curating exhibits that took what was currently trending in the contemporary art world and combined it with what was unknown and unusual. His exhibits were unexpected full-spectrum experiences, and I loved having even just a minuscule role in their execution. Art was one of the few things worth leaving the house for.

Jake was attending a lecture at the hospital that evening. He brought me to the gallery on his way, and would return for me after the lecture ended. It was my sole responsibility to let the delivery company into the gallery after hours, so they could carry in and uncrate the works. It was then up to me to place the works in the proper location according to the curator's plans, so everything was ready when Mr. Christian and the installation team arrived the following morning.

I stood just inside the gallery doors, my eyes alternating between looking down at the delivery order and looking down the street to see if the truck was coming. My thoughts overtook me. What if the delivery company had the wrong date? What if they had the wrong delivery? What if some portion of the delivery was missing or damaged? I wouldn't know what to do. The sound of the box truck's roll-up door being opened snapped me back into the present moment. I was so consumed by my thoughts that I hadn't even noticed them pull up and park. I quietly scolded myself. *Come on, Caris. Pay attention.*

The men carried the crates inside and set them all down in the center of the gallery. The driver walked over to me and asked me to sign the delivery receipt. He smelled like warm sawdust and cold sweat. I added the gallery copy of the delivery receipt to the clipboard and flipped to the placement plan. Something changed in me as I began matching up the crates to the placement plan and directing the men. I felt capable and empowered, which wasn't something I had the good fortune to feel often.

Once everything was set in place, the men swiftly unboxed the works and took the crates away. They had an incredibly streamlined process that seemed to make such light work of it. I almost wanted it to take them more time, so I could enjoy it longer. "Thank you so much, have a good night," I said with a small forced smile, as they filed out of the gallery. I locked the doors behind them. I turned on my heels to face the gallery floor, now filled with clumps of shapes, each wrapped in off-white kraft paper.

Now the real work began. I retrieved the utility knife and the rolling trash bin from the storage closet and pulled the bin behind me to the first clump of shapes. The squeak of its wheels echoed in the quiet space. I carefully slid the lever of the utility knife upward, watching the triangular blade emerge from its cold metal encasement. I found momentary amusement in the fact that I was alone with a sharp object – something my father would have never allowed.

I slowly ran the blade along the paper's edge on the first piece, popping the tape with care and being careful not to tear it, like one of those people who carefully removed the wrapping paper from gifts so they could reuse it. The first work of art had been competently extracted from its protective womb, like a child being born. I moved from piece to piece, from clump to clump, developing my own streamlined process along the way. I was disappointed to realize I'd arrived at the final clump.

I slid the blade along the paper's edge, faster and with more confidence than when I'd first begun. I held the painting by the hanging wire on the back with one hand, while I slid the kraft paper off with my other hand, adding it to the trash bin. The next steps were to identify it, inspect it for damage, and place it on the floor according to the diagram for that wall. I turned the painting around as I rested it on the floor against the wall.

I gasped at the sight of it. Panic flooded my body. I lowered myself to the floor in front of the painting, still gripping the utility knife. Everything around me became clouded and muffled, as if I were underwater. I reached out in front of me, my hands sliding down the slick surface of the painting.

I couldn't breathe.

"Life is never fair, and perhaps it is a good thing for most of us that it is not."
—Oscar Wilde

A MONTH AGO

## Jake

The first few presentations were over. The final presentation – the one I really cared about – would begin after a short break. I stood up to stretch my legs and grab a bottle of water when my phone began to buzz in my pocket. It was Caris.

"Please don't tell me you're finished already, the final presentation is just about to start."

"Jake…" She was frantic and crying.

"What is it? What's wrong?" I made my way out of the auditorium and into the hallway.

"Something terrible happened. I need you to come down here."

"Caris, tell me what happened."

"I can't…I can't tell you. I just need you to come."

I closed my eyes, raised my head toward the ceiling, and sighed. She always did this. Every time I tried to do anything outside of work, she did this. "Caris, please tell me what the problem is, and I can talk you through it over the phone, okay?"

"No," she insisted through her sobs. "I need you to come here. Please, Jake, you have to."

I paused for a moment, shaking my head in disbelief. "Alright. I'm on my way."

I knocked on the gallery doors and peered inside to find Caris sitting on the floor, her arms wrapped around her knees, her head down. She rushed to unlock the doors, flung them open, and immediately fell into my arms, burying her face into my chest, sobbing.

"It's alright," I said softly, holding her. "Tell me what happened."

Without saying a word, she took my hand and led me through the gallery, to a space in the far corner. She called my attention to the painting on the floor, leaning up against the wall. I took one look at it and understood exactly why she'd sliced it to shreds.

"Okay, here's what we're going to do..." While Caris wrote a sales order for the painting, I re-wrapped it and loaded it into the car. We finished cleaning up, locked the gallery doors behind us, and drove home in complete silence.

That night, I held Caris in my arms as we sat in front of the fireplace, sharing a glass of bourbon amidst the pungent smell of burning canvas.

## Caris

I had become nocturnal.

It was rather convenient, I suppose. We didn't have to make the typical justifi-cations for why we didn't share a bed. Jake slept at night, and I slept during the day. It was as simple as that. We never had the standard arguments that came along with cohabitating, because the entirety of our relationship had been spent in passing. Coexisting in the same location. It wasn't his fault. Or mine, really. It was just who and what we were, as different as night and day, and the longer we lived this way, the more acceptable it seemed to be.

Something happens to a person when they come near to death. It opens a door that cannot be closed. What my mother had done, nearly drowning me, opened the door between day and night, between the living and the dead. I had a mild footing on both sides of its threshold. During the day I felt like I was lost in a fog, waiting for darkness to fall, when I would know what to do with myself. At night everything became clear to me. I felt at home in the dark, among the ghosts and shadows. So I took to doing the bulk of my living during the night. I even secured an obscure role at an art gallery, supervising infrequent over-night deliveries and installations – a job nobody else showed interest in, but it was perfect for me. I loved art. If my life had gone differently, I would have studied it. I didn't care about making money. I didn't need it. The nights I went to the gallery, I existed beyond myself and the confines of my home. Someone expected something of me. That was what I needed.

I didn't enjoy food and I didn't know how to cook, so we never went out for dinner together or shared meals at home. Jake ate at the hospital most days. I survived on cold-pressed juices and protein drinks that were delivered to the house once per week by a local health food market. In the colder months, they included bone broths and teas. I couldn't remember exactly when I'd lost my interest in eating, it was a gradual transition that I wasn't conscious of for some time.

I saw Jake out the door for work every morning, then slept through the day and awoke in the early evening when he returned home. This gave me a few hours with him before he went to bed, which usually consisted of me sitting nearby while he did whatever he was going to do. I enjoyed watching him. I still felt like that same little girl with a crush on the son of my father's friend, observing him from a safe distance, content just to be near him. I was one of those small, dim, half-dead stars, fortunate enough to be positioned near one of the grandest constellations in the sky. Despite my childhood home now being the home we shared as a married couple, he was still as untouchable as he'd always been to me. He was a good husband, a devoted caregiver, and my best friend. My only friend. Trustworthy, loyal to a fault, and never unkind. He wanted absolutely nothing from me in return, and while part of me wished that he did, I was also relieved that he didn't.

While he slept during the night, I often sat in the master bedroom window seat, looking out at the stars in the dark night sky, listening to the waves crash against the cliffs at the edge of the property, and reading love stories. Stories that told me the way things should have been between us – some more explicitly than others. Sometimes I would get so caught up in what I'd read that I would remove my clothes and carefully climb into bed with him. I would get as close as I could to his body without waking him, close my eyes, and pretend we had just completed a night of passion. From just inches away, I could feel the warmth of his skin. I could breathe in his clean, spicy scent. His rhythmic breathing was as soothing to me as the waves crashing against the cliffs. Those were some of my happiest moments, but also my saddest, because I knew the truth of them. I knew that I was manufacturing those moments without his involvement or consent. I hadn't forgotten that in the beginning, we attempted to be intimate, and I just couldn't do it. We later learned that my childhood traumas had left me with a sensory disorder known as tactile defensiveness. While my mother hadn't succeeded in ending my life, in many ways, she had.

In the early morning, when darkness faded but the sun had not yet risen, I would go for a run. This was the safest time to go. The ghosts and shadows of the night followed the darkness home, but the living world had not yet begun to stir. A brief moment of true aloneness. I focused on the sound of my labored breaths, aligned with the echoing thumps of my running shoes against the pavement. I worked my way through the maze of cul-de-sacs that made up our neighborhood, lined with similar imposing manors behind tall iron gates. I wondered about the women who lived inside those homes, and how they lived their lives. Did they have careers, or children, or both? Did they take vacations and celebrate special occasions? Perhaps their lives were as solitary and uncelebrated as my own. Maybe all marriages ended up in the place mine had always been, and we weren't so out of the ordinary, but rather ahead of our time. While part of me would find comfort in assigning some normalcy to the way we lived, I would not wish this way of life upon any other woman. I could feel another version of myself inside of me, trying to fight her way to the surface, desperately wanting the life she'd been denied.

I had come to know my running path well, and the exact number of steps and breaths it took to complete it. Routine was a useful tool in keeping me stable. I ended each run at the back of the property, standing on the edge of the cliff, looking down at the unforgiving path to the bottom. I would take one step backward from the edge for each thing I could find to be grateful for, knowing full well that the day I could no longer find a reason to take a step backward would be the day I took a step forward.

I plucked a few flower stems on my way through the gardens to the back door, to refresh the arrangement that always stood in the center of the kitchen island. I showered and dressed for the day while the coffee brewed, so by the time Jake made his way downstairs for work I was ready to see him off. I always turned my head as I handed him his travel mug, so he knew I anticipated a kiss on the cheek. He reluctantly obliged, without fail. I did my hair and makeup, and put on nice clothes, just for this brief interaction each morning.

Once he was gone, I locked the door, took my pills, and went upstairs to sleep. The pills kept my mind still. Without them, my subconscious would take me to all sorts of places I didn't want to go. Places that were sometimes difficult to return from. I always slept on my back with my hands clasped in front of me, with my clothes, shoes, and makeup on, and never under the covers. If one day my consciousness failed to return to my body, this would make light work of preparing my corpse for burial.

## SUNDAY MORNING

### *Jake*

I could still smell the warm scent of her, mixed with the cool evening breeze, as I made my way into the hospital that morning. I couldn't be certain if still having her purse in my possession somehow played a part in her ability to communicate with me through my dreams, so I thought it might be best to hold onto it for the time being. I now had a way to identify her without it.

I sat down in the neurology office, logged into the computer system, and checked her case file for updates. Conjugate eye movements, just like those occurring during the REM portion of the sleep cycle, had been observed consistently overnight. This meant her brain was operating at the same level it would be if she were awake. No other changes had been noted. She had not yet regained consciousness. *What was she waiting for?*

I scrolled through my inbox and located the email about the most recent hospital lecture series. I printed the page featuring her lecture on the nature of human consciousness, which included a photo and bio, and added it to her patient file, then updated her patient name. She was no longer a Jane Doe.

I pulled up the website for Meridian Gallery. It was closed on Sundays. There was a photo of Dexter Christian on the contact page, exactly as he appeared in my dream. This was truly remarkable. I needed to let him know that she was here in the hospital, but first I needed to look for something that would connect them. I couldn't exactly tell him that I received his name in a dream, or from the contents of her purse that I'd failed to turn in.

I closed the door to her hospital room and left the lights off as I had the day before. Gray and rainy mornings always felt muted and introspective, even at the hospital. Everything was tinged with a sense of quiet calm, and the world seemed to move a little bit slower. Raindrops gently tapped on the window, creating a soothing, rhythmic sound that calmed my nerves.

"Good morning, Alaina, it's Jake," I leaned back in the bedside chair next to her. "I hope you're able to hear me. It's early Sunday morning. It's raining to-day. You're doing much better than the last time I sat next to you in the rain… Thank you for everything you shared with me last night. I was able to provide the hospital with your identity this morning, and I'm going to reach Dexter Christian as soon as possible to let him know you're here."

I wasn't able to locate any personal social media accounts for Dexter Christian, just a public Instagram account for Meridian Gallery. I began scrolling through the posts, hoping to find a photo of Alaina and Dexter together. There was nothing, but I did see that Alaina had interacted with a few of the posts. I clicked on her name, but her profile was set to private. I switched to Google and searched for Alaina M. Ryan. There was a lot out there in reference to her research work, but nothing pertaining to her personal life.

I set down my phone and leaned in. "On the one hand, I love that you're not plastered all over social media. On the other hand, that makes my task all the more difficult. You weren't wearing an engagement ring or a wedding band, but I'm not sure that means what it used to. I have a wife. Caris. I do love her, but not the way a husband should love his wife. All I ever wanted was to marry the love of my life and build a family together. As much as I want to be a father, I think it's for the best that Caris and I don't have children. It's all I can manage to protect her from herself, let alone protect our children from her. Sometimes I wish I could go back in time and make a different choice. I wonder how different my life would be if I had."

I kept pausing for a response, like I would in any other conversation. I kept hoping she would take one of those moments to open her eyes and say something to me. Instead, the slow beeping of the monitors punctuated the silence within every pause. Today I had no plan other than to keep sitting here and keep talking to her. The rest of the hospital could get on without me.

"When my brother and I were growing up, our parents took us to a lot of museums. Once, we went to a special exhibit on the Egyptian pyramids, and I was so fascinated by it. They even had a real mummy in a sarcophagus. I got as close as I could to the glass and examined every detail. That night I had the best dream, one of the only dreams I can ever remember having. I dreamed that I lived all alone inside a pyramid, full of books to read, games to play, and treasures to sift through. I spent so much time thinking about that dream, wishing it would come true. Now when I think about that dream, I realize it did come true. I live in a sealed tomb full of stale air and old valuables that don't belong to me, and I share it with a corpse.

I can't stop thinking about the moment I first saw you walking across the street. The moment our eyes met, something happened between us. The way you were looking back at me, I think you felt the same thing. I wish I would have gotten to the bookstore just a few minutes earlier, or not gone to the coffeehouse first. I wish I would have done any number of things differently that morning so that this might not have happened to you. I'm not sure if I actually believe in fate, but if there is such a thing, then maybe there's nothing I could have done differently that would have changed anything. I can't understand how someone like you could be assigned such a fate, when so many people live long and healthy lives without ever making good use of themselves. It just doesn't seem fair, does it?

I'm choosing to believe that you reached out to me because you want a way back to your life, because you still have things you want to understand and experience. I trust that you've got a good reason for not coming back just yet, but I need you to understand that the longer you choose to stay away, the less chance you have of coming back. You know, I've been doing nothing but surviving for as long as I can remember. Just keeping my head down, working hard, focusing on the needs of others, and getting myself from one day to the next. I thought it was the best I could do. And then you showed up. You showed up, and in an ordinary instant, changed everything I thought I knew. You've made me want to do so much more than survive, and you've reminded me that I deserve to."

## SUNDAY AFTERNOON
## Jake

The entire morning had escaped me. I left her room to stretch my legs, hit the bathroom, and grab something to eat. On my way to the cafeteria, I noticed *The Midnight Library* displayed in the window of the hospital gift shop. I had to buy it. I had to read the book she told me she loved. I couldn't wait to get back to her room and start reading it to her. Maybe that would get her to open her eyes. I decided at that moment I was going to fight for her. I was going to be the one watching over her, keeping her company, keeping her safe. I would be the hand she felt and the voice she heard. I would be there, all day, every day, for as long as it took. It felt more right to me than any choice I'd ever made.

I couldn't fix Caris. I did my best to understand her and what she needed. The people who cared about me did their best to understand why I tolerated the loneliness, frustration, and isolation that was my life with her. I could never let people in too far, or tell them too much. It always led to the question, *why do you stay?* I had to stay. It was an obligation I'd been forced to take on, and I could never tell another living soul the reasons why. No one would believe me if I did.

I couldn't fix Alaina. There was no medical reason for her continued cataleptic state. I'd been over and over her case file, and so had others. This was a choice she was making, and I wanted to understand why. I wanted to help her with whatever she was facing that kept her from returning to her life.

I returned to her room and slumped into the bedside chair, exhausted. I opened the book and began to read.

Our texts began immediately following Alaina's return to New York and became almost a daily occurrence. Before long, we graduated to phone or video calls three evenings per week. We never ran out of things to talk about, and there was nothing we couldn't say to each other. She was so easy to talk to. I could hardly remember what my life was like before she was a part of it, and I didn't want to.

"The hospital has its annual fundraiser coming up at the end of the month. I'm expected to go. I wondered if you might want to go with me. I know you don't have plans to head back this way, but I thought I'd at least ask."

"I would be happy to come back to Chicago just to be your date for the fundraiser."

"Seriously? You would do that?"

"Of course."

"That would be amazing, thank you. We could make a weekend of it, if you wanted. I can get you a hotel room, or you're welcome to stay with me if you'd be comfortable with that. I'd give you my bedroom of course, and I'll take the couch."

Alaina texted me from the car to let me know she was ten minutes away. Dex picked her up from the airport that afternoon so they could spend a little time together before he drove to Michigan to pay a long overdue visit to his mother. I got the impression he avoided going home, but his mother had been unwell and Alaina convinced him it was time to go.

"Are you sure about this?" Dex asked as he pulled her suitcase from the trunk of the car.

"I'll be just fine. If I didn't trust him, I wouldn't be here."

He reached down to hug her. "Text me now and then so I know you're doing alright. If you need me, I can be back here in less than two hours."

"Everything will be fine, Dex, try to enjoy yourself. Give Gloria a hug for me, and tell her I hope she's feeling better soon. I'll see you in a few days."

Dex waited for Alaina to enter the building before pulling away. I met her in the lobby and immediately took her into my arms. We'd spent so many hours talking and texting since our first date, that it didn't feel at all like we'd only spent one day together before. She was more familiar to me than people I'd known my whole life.

"I missed you," I whispered to her.

"I missed you, too."

"Let me get that for you," I reached down and took her suitcase, motioning toward the elevator.

My loft was several floors up and had a gorgeous view of Lake Michigan. The kitchen, dining area, and living room were all one large space. It had dark wood floors and brick exterior walls with large floor-to-ceiling windows. There was a dark brown leather couch with a matching oversized chair and ottoman, which sat across from a large flat-screen TV on the only interior wall. There were two bedrooms, one large and one small, connected by a shared bathroom. I used the small bedroom as a storage and workout space. The whole place was very minimal, organized, and clean.

While Alaina got ready for bed in the bathroom, I put on my sleeping clothes, turned down the bed for her, and placed a bottle of water on the nightstand. I grabbed a spare pillow and blanket from the smaller bedroom and headed for the couch. Alaina came out of the bathroom and said goodnight on her way to my bedroom.

The leather couch was really uncomfortable and produced a symphony of embarrassing creaks and grunts as I tried to find a position I could sleep in – noises I hoped she would not hear and think were coming from me.

"Jake?" she whispered from the bedroom doorway.

*Shit. She heard.* "Hey, are you okay? Do you need anything?"

"No, I'm fine, but I can tell you're not comfortable out here. Please, come share the bed with me."

"Are you sure?"

"I'm sure. It's your bed, after all."

We talked for a while, about everything under the sun, before falling asleep beside each other. I'd never slept better than I did next to her.

The Art Institute of Chicago was one of the places Alaina had always wanted to go, so I made sure to take her there. We got there right when it opened, and other than a children's art class, we had the place to ourselves. We slowly walked through the museum, hand in hand. Every once in a while I would raise her hand to my lips and kiss it. She was in awe of the many famous works she had never seen in person before. Picasso. Renoir. Monet. Chagall. I was in awe of *her*.

We sat down together on the bench in front of *America Windows* by Marc Chagall, a trio of stained glass windows featuring a tapestry of symbols celebrating American life, art, and history. The windows cast a heavenly blue glow throughout the otherwise dark room.

"I always thought Chagall was a painter," I said. "I never knew he worked with stained glass."

"He didn't. Chagall created the design, but someone else assembled the construct," she said in a hushed voice, as if she were in church. Maybe she was. "Then it was returned to him, so he could paint what he envisioned within the borders of the construct. I like to think of it as a metaphor for life. While we all start with a plan for our lives, we aren't in control of how it comes together. All we can do is paint the most beautiful experiences we can, within the parameters we've received."

My parents brought us here many times while we were growing up, but I never really thought about what the art meant, just whether or not I liked how it looked. I understood exactly what she was saying to me. I was ready to understand it now. I wanted so badly to tell her how much I loved her, and how she changed the way I saw art, the world, and myself, but it didn't feel like the right time.

From out of nowhere, an adorable little girl was unexpectedly standing in front of us. She began frantically signing. Thankfully, Alaina knew sign language. She signed back in return, speaking out loud as she did so, to give me some idea of what was happening.

"It's nice to meet you, Emma. My name is Alaina, and this is Jake. Jake, I'm going to help Emma find the ladies' room. Would you please find Emma's mother and let her know she's safe?"

"You bet," I replied, heading off in the opposite direction.

I was standing near the entrance to the art studio with the class instructor and Emma's mother when Alaina came down the hallway with Emma skipping along at her side, and waving to her mother.

"Thank you so much," Emma's mother said. "She was determined to go all by herself and insisted she knew the way. It was very kind of you to help her."

"It was my pleasure," Alaina replied with a warm smile. Emma turned to Alaina and signed to her once more. "Emma would like to show me her painting if that's alright with you."

"Of course," I replied. Emma took Alaina's hand and pulled her into the art studio.

"Your wife is lovely," Emma's mother said. I loved hearing Alaina referred to as my wife so much that I didn't bother to correct her. I watched through the open doors of the studio as she knelt in the center of the group of children, all eager to show her their paintings. She took the time to look at each one and say something complimentary. Lovely was the perfect word to describe her.

We finished our tour of the museum, stopped for lunch, and then finished the day at my favorite place in Chicago, The Field Museum of Natural History, before heading back to the loft to get ready for the hospital fundraiser.

I woke up, disoriented, in the chair beside her bed. I grabbed my phone and searched *America Windows* by Marc Chagall. It was part of the permanent collection at The Art Institute of Chicago, and was recently restored, courtesy of a grant from The Ryan Foundation. I followed the link to The Ryan Foundation website, where Alaina and Dexter were pictured together. Below the photo, the caption read: *Alaina Ryan, founder of The Ryan Foundation, with her godfather, Dexter Christian, owner and curator of Meridian Gallery, Chicago.*

She had led me directly to the connection I needed to contact Dexter Christian immediately.

"Character is higher than intellect. A great soul will be strong to live as well as think." —Ralph Waldo Emerson

SUNDAY NIGHT

## Jake

I entered the bedroom to find Caris sitting in the window seat, legs curled under her, a throw blanket wrapped around her shoulders like a shawl. She had moved the small round table from the sitting area to the window and set up the chess board while I was in the shower.

"Please, will you play a quick game with me before you go to sleep? I've barely seen you the last few days."

"Sure," I reluctantly agreed. I just wanted to go to bed. I sat down in the window seat, on the opposite side of the board. Caris was grinning like a child, thrilled that I had agreed to play with her. "Ladies first."

She moved her king pawn two spaces, immediately attacking the center. "How was your day?"

"Much quieter, which allowed me to spend my time working on a unique case," I matched her opening move.

"What kind of unique case?"

"A woman in a coma," I always told her the truth, but I purposely limited the details. "There is no medical reason she should still be unconscious, and yet, she is." I moved my knight cautiously. She already had me cornered.

Caris moved her bishop diagonally, capturing one of my pawns. She grinned for a moment, pleased with herself, but returned with a much more serious expression. A shadow fell over her face, drawing attention to her harsh bone structure, emphasized by the moonlight coming in through the window. She could be truly unsettling at times. I chose to study the board instead, carefully considering my next move, realizing my options were now limited.

"What happened?" I'd left myself wide open. She moved her rook to threaten my queen.

I couldn't be certain if she was referring to the patient or the game. "To the patient? She was hit by a car."

I moved my king, not to safety, but into the only position that gave my queen a fighting chance. At that moment, I realized something. The queen could move in any direction, she was not limited to just one space. She could move freely, as long as she was not obstructed.

Alaina was waiting for me when I arrived at the White Plains airport. It felt liberating to be out of Chicago, away from the hospital, and with her. She showed me everything she loved about upstate New York on the way back to her family home, where she gave me my first cooking lesson as we made dinner together. After an amazing dinner, we sat down on the sofa in front of the fireplace and opened a bottle of wine. The occasional burst of cool night air washing in from the open windows felt amazing in contrast to the warmth of the fire.

"Did you have a good day?" She nestled into the back of the sofa on her side to face me.

"I had an incredible day. How was your day?"

"It was perfect. I spent it in my favorite place, with my favorite person. The moon is full. The tides are turning. Nothing could make this day more perfect."

"Hold that thought." Moments later, I returned with a large, shallow box tied with a wide satin ribbon, placing it on her lap. "Open it." I could not contain my grin.

Alaina set down her glass of wine and slid the ribbon from the box, removing the cover and tucking it underneath the bottom. She folded the two flaps of tissue paper outward to reveal a framed photograph. She gazed at it in disbelief. "This can't be what it looks like…"

"I told my parents all about you, how wonderful you are, and how it feels like I've known you my whole life. It turns out, my dad and your granddad were friends. Our families spent the day together once. This was taken at Navy Pier." My index finger hovered above the glass as I moved from person to person in the photo. "Your parents, my parents, my brother, me…and there you are. You must have been about four years old."

"I don't know what to say."

"I brought the rest of the photos they had from that day," I removed a small stack of photos from the bottom of the box. "Your granddad is in some of the others. He must have taken this one."

Alaina looked carefully at each photo, moving it to the back of the stack as she looked at the next. "How long have you known about this?"

"A few weeks. Are you upset that I didn't tell you right away?"

"No. You were right to tell me this in person, and you did so in such a lovely, thoughtful way. But you've had some time with this... What have you been thinking?"

"Honestly, I think this validates what we already knew. That we belong together. I think this is why no one else has ever felt like home, for either of us."

"Soulmates," she whispered. A tear fell slowly down her cheek as she looked into my eyes. I leaned forward and gently wiped the tear from her cheek before kissing her softly.

"Wait," she stopped and pulled away. She went to the bookcase and searched the rows, tipping a dark leather-bound book forward by the top of its spine. She removed it from the shelf and returned to the sofa. "This is my mother's journal from that year. I want to see what she wrote on that day.

In the first entry of her first journal, she wrote that a journal contains your most personal and private thoughts and feelings, and her inner monologue would always speak French. My father gave her the same journal every Christmas to use the coming year. I have all twelve of them, one for each year they had together. She didn't journal the last four years of her life. She stopped the day he died, and pottery became her daily obsession. Here it is, her entry from that day..." She read the entry out loud for me, in English.

*Today was our first full day in Chicago with John's father. Alaina has been unwell the last 24 hours, as she always is following a long bout of travel. I hope one day we can understand this for her, so she might feel well as she explores the world. I know that she will do so regardless, as she has already proven herself to be far too curious and determined to spend her life all in one place. She is like me in that way, and in most other ways she takes after her father.*

*There was an Independence Day celebration at Navy Pier today, for Naval officers and their families. John's father took us there, along with his good friend, his wife, and their two young sons. Alaina was fussy and I could not seem to soothe her. Their youngest had a way with her, and Alaina was quite taken with him. That provided her with some distraction, and me with some relief from her constant care. She would much rather be in her father's arms than mine, but I hoped to give him today with his father. He will not be with us much longer.*

"There is no chance, no destiny, no fate,
that can circumvent or hinder or control the
firm resolve of a determined soul."
—Ella Wheeler Wilcox

# SUNDAY NIGHT

## Alaina

Dewy blades of grass tickled my ankles as I walked barefoot through the front lawn of the imposing stone manor. The property was surrounded by a closed iron gate. I wasn't sure how I'd gotten through the gate and onto the front lawn. Why was I here? The sun had not yet risen, there was just the dim, gray light that existed somewhere between night and day. The meticulously maintained front gardens were both vibrant and fragrant, but much more manicured than my gardens at home. There was a harshness to them, a strictness. They inexplicably flourished amid dull hardscapes with so much barren space in between them. They thrived, despite their living conditions.

I leaped from the wet grass onto a stone path leading around the side of the house. The cold morning air washed across my skin as the thin fabric of my hospital gown fluttered with my movements, sending chills through me. My goosebumps were so pronounced, they made my skin hurt. I was beyond exposed. Beyond vulnerable. My bare feet scraped along the cold, coarse stone beneath them as I came to a large window on the patio, its sill above my stature. I stepped onto the stone railing that surrounded the patio – a border not high enough to keep anyone in or out, a border that existed solely to send the message of unwelcome.

I was weak and unsteady. My fingers ached as they clung to the jagged stone exterior. I strained to peer through the very bottom of the window, through the diamond-shaped leading atop the glass. What am I here to see? There was a woman seated inside, at a long wooden table, in the chair nearest to the window. She was alone, staring across the table at no one, as if in a trance. She was well-dressed, her blonde hair pulled back into a sleek low bun. She was plain, but pretty. Pale. She wore no makeup, except for deep red lipstick that did not suit her. Her lips begged to be noticed, while the rest of her begged to be ignored.

My fingers turned white from both the cold temperature and the strain of holding myself in position on the ledge. I lost my balance. I looked down for just a moment to regain my footing, and when I looked up again, the woman was no longer at the table. I lowered myself down, clinging to the side of the house for stability. When I turned around to leave, the woman was standing directly behind me. She glared at me, arms folded, in her perfectly pressed gray dress pants and boring shoes, her sleeveless turtleneck a creamy bisque color just like my mother's pottery. Quickly, suddenly, she reached out and grabbed ahold of me, one hand tightly gripping my arm and the other on the back of my neck, as she flung me through the open door and into the kitchen.

I fell to the floor and slid into the base of the wooden table. I used the nearest chair to bring myself to my feet, and when I turned around both she and the door were gone. I looked out the window to find her standing on the front lawn, arms at her sides, hair in disarray around her shoulders, barefooted and wearing my hospital gown. I looked down at myself, realizing I was standing there in her clothes, arms folded, my dark hair pulled back into a sleek low bun. I rushed forward, placing my clammy palms against the cold glass, and watched her run for her life, through the wet grass, away from this place.

She was free now. She was free, and I was not.

I quickly turned and looked around the stark, still space. The kitchen was bare and impeccably clean, as if it had never been cooked in. There was no warmth inside, it was just as bitingly cold as it had been outside, except for a bright and beautiful vase of flowers in the center of the island. I banged my fists against the thick window glass, until I became light-headed. I lowered myself into the chair where I had first seen her sitting, staring across the table at no one, as everything faded to black.

## MONDAY MORNING

### Jake

Anger swelled within me as I realized I had once again woken up alone, to a life I hated, to a life without her. It took every ounce of self-control I had not to trash the bedroom.

I returned to the hospital, hoping for a miracle. Hoping that I would walk into that room and find her awake, sitting up and waiting to greet me, waiting to tell me that dream wasn't just mine. I once again entered the room to find her unconscious. The bland and sterile room contrasted sharply with the vibrant soul asleep within it. Seeing her like this, so still and lifeless, filled me with such frustration. It wasn't just me who was missing out on knowing her. The whole world was.

I quietly sat with her, replaying the dreams over and over again in my mind. The only place where we could be free from the obstacles and complications that plagued our realities, my dreams were both a blessing and a curse, giving me a glimpse of complete contentment with the woman I was meant to be with, while stressing the painful gap between what might have been and the harsh reality of what was. I took bittersweet comfort in the reminder that she was still alive, she was still here, but that my only recourse was to sit there beside her and hope, beg, and plead for an outcome I could live with.

"Life and death are one thread, the same line viewed from different sides."
—Lao Tzu

MONDAY NIGHT

## Jake

I searched the entire house for her. She wasn't there. I hurried to the master bedroom window that overlooked the back of the property. There were no lights on in the carriage house or the greenhouse. Out of the corner of my eye, I caught a glimpse of a shadow moving near the back gate. I rushed from the bedroom, through the house, to the back door. I shouted her name as I flew down the concrete steps and down the narrow blacktop drive that led to the carriage house. It was bitterly cold. *Alaina! Alaina, please wait!*

When I reached the back gate, it was open, and banging against the closure in the high winds. She had to be headed for the cliffs. It was even colder at the water's edge, and the waves would be crashing violently against the rocky shoreline. This wasn't safe. She had to stop. She had to let me bring her back to the house, though that was the last place I ever wanted her to be.

Her long hair and her hospital gown had both been taken by the wind and clung tightly to one side of her. I called to her again. *Alaina!* This time she looked over her shoulder at me, just as she took a step forward and disappeared over the edge. I watched her fall in slow motion, drifting further away from me.

I awoke, mercifully, before I had to watch her reach the bottom. I was drenched in a cold sweat, my heart pounding in my chest. I wiped my eyes and looked around the room, trying to get my bearings. This was not at all like the other dreams. *Why would I dream of her here?* I never wanted her to be anywhere near this place. I never wanted a piece of my awful reality to get close to her.

The dream was so vivid, so real, that I was concerned it had been a premonition. I couldn't stop seeing her face, sad yet serene, accepting, as she left my line of sight over the edge of the cliff. The finality of it, the gut-wrenching sense of loss, was unbearable.

I rushed to the bedroom window and looked toward the back gate, debating if I should rush down to the cliffs. *Did I honestly expect to find her out there?* She was lying in a hospital bed across town. This was not our goodbye. I was not going to let that happen.

The cold air was biting at my skin as I raced to the garage. The dream replayed in my mind over and over again. I couldn't shake her peaceful expression as she slipped away, and the emptiness I felt watching it unfold in front of me, powerless to stop it. I tried to convince myself that it was just a dream, nothing more, but a voice in the back of my mind, persistent and insistent, kept telling me otherwise. *What if it wasn't just a dream? What if I'd already lost her?*

The hospital was only a short drive away, but it felt like an eternity. Every second that passed fed my worst fear, that when I got there, it would already be too late. I gripped the steering wheel so tightly that it made my hands ache as I sped through the dark, quiet streets. I quickly turned off the annoying overnight talk radio show. Now only my own heavy breaths were audible to me. My frantic thoughts came in fragments. Split-second flashes of the dream pulsated in front of my eyes as I drove. I was paying little attention to traffic laws, there was nobody out here at this hour anyway. The only word capable of escaping my tightly clenched jaw was please. Over and over, I whispered, please.

I reached the hospital entrance and left my truck under the valet canopy with the keys inside. The bright white lights of the hospital interior pierced my eyes as I ran through it, headed straight for the first bank of elevators. Frantically, I pushed the upward arrows on all four elevators, positioning myself in the center to rush to whichever set of doors might open first.

*Please. Please. Please.*

This was taking too long. I caught someone coming through the nearby stair-well door and decided that was the way to go. I pushed the slowly closing door hard enough to hit the wall behind it and crack the window glass. I grabbed the cold metal handrail and pulled myself up the first flight of stairs, skipping as many steps as I could, swung myself around the turn, and pulled myself up the next flight, again and again, until I reached the long-term care floor.

Without stopping to catch my breath, I flung open the stairwell door and start-ed down the hallway to her room. The patient floors were more dimly lit than the common areas this time of night. The sound of my shoes slapping against the hard linoleum echoed as I ran through the empty distance of the hallway. Nobody was sitting at the nurse's station. The door to her room was closed. I looked down at the door handle as I gripped it, closing my eyes for just a mo-ment as I took a deep breath. I slowly pulled open the door.

*Please. Please. Please.*

A man was standing in the room, in front of the window, looking out. For a moment, I thought it might be Dex. He turned toward the door as he heard me come in. I glanced at the hospital bed to my left, out of the corner of my eye. It was empty. The machinery was removed from the room. The bed was stripped down to the bare mattress. The strong smell of hospital-grade disinfectant filled my nostrils and burned my throat – the kind of product hospitals used to clean up after surgeries and deaths.

*Please, God, no. She can't be gone.*

"Are you Dr. Matthews?"

His question ripped me from my thoughts and into the present. Keep it together, I told myself. "Yes, I am. How can I help you?"

"David Hillstrom. I'm an investigator. I'm told you were present during the hit and run of the woman who was in this room."

He handed me his card. I took it from him without looking at it. "Yes, I was. I assisted her in the street and waited with her until the ambulance arrived."

"I see. I know it's late, but would you be willing to come with me to answer a few questions? I just need a bit more information, then we can wrap this up."

"Of course, whatever you need."

"Thank you, I appreciate that. Shall we?" He motioned toward the door. "I hope you don't mind taking this elsewhere. I'm not really a fan of hospitals. No offense." When we reached the bank of elevators, he pressed the lobby button.

*Stay calm. If he thought you were guilty of something, you'd be in handcuffs right now.* "Wrap this up...does that mean you've located the driver?" We walked through the lobby and out the front entrance of the hospital.

"They turned themselves in, actually."

I watched two uniformed officers take possession of my truck as I got into the investigator's car with him. My mind raced. *Why were they taking my truck?* I tried desperately to choke down my emotions. I needed to maintain my composure here, my professionalism. All I wanted to do was cry. Grieve. To talk to her, wherever she was now. I wanted to look up at the constellations in the dark night sky and tell her that *I* was the one who was dying when we met. That moment on the street instantly changed the course of my life, and I would be forever grateful to her.

"So, what brought you to the hospital in the middle of the night tonight?"

A fair question that I did not have a fair answer to. I couldn't exactly tell him I was brought here by a nightmare. "Maggie, one of the overnight nurses, texted to let me know you were waiting there to speak with me."

"Ah. How well did you know her? The victim." He glanced at me while keeping his focus on the road.

"I didn't know her at all." I hated having to say those words, but they were true. As well as I felt like I knew her, all of those moments existed only within my dreams.

He seemed confused by my answer. "The nurses stated you visited her every day, sometimes more than once. Do you always take a special interest in good looking coma patients you don't know?"

Man, he was tough. I couldn't help but notice we were not headed in the direction of the police station, or the direction of the house. We were headed North on Sheridan Road, along the lakeshore, toward the old Grosse Point Lighthouse. *Where was he taking me?* I turned my head toward him as I began to answer his question, noticing the handle of a holstered gun peeking out from the left side of his sports jacket.

"As a neurologist, I have an interest in coma cases in general, which we don't see very often around here. She provided an opportunity to study the cognitive and communicative abilities of the unconscious mind. Any neurologist would jump at that chance. She might have emerged from the coma at any time, so I visited as often as I could, even if that meant keeping strange hours for a while." While I spoke, I pulled his business card from my pocket. He was not with the police department, he was a private investigator.

"What are some of those capabilities? Just out of curiosity, if you don't mind me asking."

"Some patients have awakened from comas having experienced moments of awareness mixed with lucid dreaming, unable to distinguish between the two. Others have claimed to have visited alternative timelines and realities while having some kind of out-of-body experience. The patients awakened with full memories of places they had never physically been. There have been people who dreamed of speaking to the patient, and the patient awoke with full knowledge of that conversation."

We passed the service road that led to Grosse Point Lighthouse and Lighthouse Beach, then passed the road that led to Lawson Park. My brother and I had hiked out here before, but never this far North. From here the woods became denser and teeming with dangerous wildlife, with cliffs that dropped off into one of the roughest parts of Lake Michigan. There were a lot of shipwrecks out here before the lighthouse was built.

"You don't really believe in all that shit, do you?" he smirked. "I mean, as a man of science?"

"It defies logic, to be sure, but the first-hand accounts of these types of experiences are extensive. There has to be something to it, I just don't know what it is. Like you, I ask questions and try to get to the truth of things."

"Fair enough," he nodded in agreement.

"Who did you say hired you?" I asked, as casually as I could manage.

He smiled and declined to answer. "We're here."

The car slowed as it approached an unmarked road on the right. Gravel crunched under the tires as we slowly passed underneath a massive iron archway that read: Orrington Asylum. I had no idea this place was out here. *Why would we be here? Was she alive, and the hospital had her moved here? Is this why she took me to the cliffs, not those at the back of the property, but here to let me know where she was taken?*

The tall stone building had an ominous feel to it, with its sharp pointed towers and arched windows. It wasn't unlike the Carlisle house, maybe this was the location of the dream. The iron plaque embedded into the stonework at the base of the entrance said: Orrington Seminary, 1863. We walked into the lobby with its original tiled floors, thick woodwork, and iron-clad windows. I followed Hillstrom to the information desk, positioned behind a tall wooden counter with glass partitions.

The woman behind the counter raised her head and smiled. "Good evening, Mr. Hillstrom. Dr. Matthews. We're all ready for you. This way, please."

We entered a small, plain meeting room not far from the information desk. It was painted a pale green color that matched the floor tiles, with a small wooden table and chairs in the center of it. No windows, not even a clock on its bare plaster walls. It may as well have been an interrogation room at the police station. There was a single file folder waiting for us in the middle of the table, and two bottles of water.

"Have a seat. I hope you don't mind us doing this here. Two birds, one stone, I figured. It's late. I'm sure we'd both like to get this taken care of so we can head home."

"Of course," I replied. "Though, I'm not still sure what *this* is."

"Let's get right to it, then. Dr. Matthews, did you see the vehicle that struck the woman you helped in the street?"

"No, I did not. I was focused on assisting the woman. Once I had done all I could for her, I scanned the area for additional victims. I asked the witnesses gathered around me if the driver needed help, and if there was anyone else in the vehicle. I was told the vehicle never stopped."

"So you're saying, you had no idea it was your own vehicle that ran down the victim?"

"My own vehicle? No. That's not possible."

"And why is that?"

"I rode my motorcycle that day."

Hillstrom opened the file folder and pulled out three photographs, displaying them on the table in front of me like a blackjack dealer. "These were taken by security cameras in the immediate area at the time of the hit and run. Is this your vehicle, Dr. Matthews? The one you drove to the hospital tonight?"

I looked down at the photos confidently, certain it could not possibly be my vehicle in them. I hoped one of them would show my motorcycle parked at the curb in front of the bookstore, and that none of them would show me walking away with her purse.

It was definitely my vehicle in the photos. My license plate. My state park sticker was in the lower corner of the windshield. There was the small dent left behind by the coyote my brother and I narrowly avoided killing on our way back from a hiking trip. "Yes," I replied. "I'm not sure how it's possible, but yes, this is my vehicle."

"And you're certain you did not know the victim?"

"No. I'd never seen her before."

He sifted through the remaining pages in the folder, producing a printout with the Northwestern Medical logo at the top and handing it to me. "Are you sure? She gave a lecture at your hospital about a month ago. Your name is on the attendance list."

"I did attend an earlier lecture that evening, but was called away before the main presentation. My wife had an emergency."

Hillstrom pulled out the last photo in the folder and placed it on top of the others, tapping down on it with his index finger. "Can you identify the person driving your vehicle in this photo?"

I lowered my eyes to the photo, wanting to know, and also not wanting to know. "Yes," I pinched the bridge of my nose, closed my eyes, and shook my head in disbelief. I could barely choke out the words. "That's my wife." The atmosphere of the room completely changed.

"To answer your earlier question, Dr. Matthews, I was hired by your father-in-law. The police got in touch with Dr. Carlisle after your wife was arrested. He insisted that she be admitted immediately for a full psychiatric evaluation. As her husband, the facility asked that you please sign that authorization form as well, just as a formality." He slid the paper toward me and produced a pen from his shirt pocket.

I began reading over the document. "Can he do that?"

"He has power of attorney. He's also a major benefactor with a seat on the board of directors, so yes, I'd say he can. Besides, it was this or prison. This is all pretty cut and dry, as far as the police are concerned. I'm sure you noticed they took possession of your vehicle once it was located. Did your wife ever mention anything to you about the hit and run?"

"No. Not a word," I signed the form.

"That didn't seem unusual to you?"

"No, not really. Caris kept a lot of secrets. Can I see her? Talk to her?"

"Unfortunately not, I'm sorry. The hospital insists on no contact during the evaluation process. I do have one more thing for you to sign, as well as an envelope from your father-in-law," He slid the document across the table. "It looks like you're getting a do-over." *Declaration of Nullity of Marriage.* Caris had already signed it. I added my signature to the document and pushed it back to him. I tore open the sealed envelope from my father-in-law and pulled out the note card. Caris's wedding ring, which had once belonged to my grand-mother, slid from the envelope and pinged as it hit the desk.

*Jake,*

*This was inevitable, I think we both know that. The balance of the shared bank account remains yours. Please vacate the house as soon as you are able. Your responsibilities end here. Thank you for all you have done for my daughter.*

*Charles Carlisle*

# FRIDAY MORNING

## Caris

I heard the motorcycle rumble its way down the long blacktop driveway from the carriage house where Jake stored it. I watched from the front window, my arms folded, leaning up against the casing so he couldn't catch me. I did know how much he loved to ride. I did know how seldom he had the chance. Still, I couldn't shake the feeling that there was more to this.

"That's because there is..." My mother stood in the doorway at the other end of the room. She had one arm on the door frame, the other on her hip, posed like she was being photographed for the swimsuit issue of a magazine. Her long, dark hair sat in wet clumps, resting on her shoulders. She smelled of chlorine.

"Why are you still here?" I asked angrily.

She took a few steps into the room, toward me. I had no way to leave the room without walking right past her. "Because *you're* still here, Caris. Until the world is rid of you, I can't have my freedom. None of us can."

I started to cry. "I don't understand. Why did you try to kill me? Why are you so desperate to rid the world of me? Mothers are supposed to love their daughters. Protect them. Care for them."

"You're a monster, Caris. Do you really not know that? It was my responsibility to correct the mistake I made by bringing you into this world. Your father was weak. Blind. All he could see was his little girl. He didn't have the strength to do what needed to be done. It was up to me to find the strength, and to pay the price for it. He sent me away and found a caregiver willing to contain you in this place until you were of age."

"Of age for what?"

"Marrying age, Caris. Are you really so foolish? Your father was plotting his escape from you. He gave you what you wanted. He pressed Jake into marrying you and then fled as far as he could from you," she looked around the room. "He handed you the keys to your own prison and hand-selected your warden. None of this was to keep you safe. It was to keep everyone else safe from you."

"No…That isn't true. Jake loves me."

"Wake up, Caris. Jake is out there right now, plotting his own escape from you." Water dripped from her hand as she pointed out the window toward the street. "He's using his time away from you to build a new life with someone else, far away from you. Just as your father did."

I gathered up the courage to run past her, down the short hallway that led to the kitchen. I could hear her laughing from the other room as I frantically searched for the keys to the truck. I vaguely knew how to drive. I didn't have a license. But there was no time to call for a taxi, I needed to get downtown and stop this immediately. I found the spare key fob in the drawer by the back door. I flung the door open and ran through the side yard, to the main garage.

I got into the driver's seat, closed the door, and brought the seatbelt over me. I remembered from watching Jake, the button on the upper left would open the overhead garage door. I put my foot on the brake and pushed the ignition button as the door began to rise, letting sunlight into the cold, dark space. I squinted. I saw my mother in the window, looking at me, amused by how clumsy and clueless I was. I knew I needed to put the car in drive, but the gear shift would only move into neutral. It took me a moment to realize I needed to push in the small button on the side of it to make it move. I shifted the truck into drive and gripped the steering wheel with both hands, slowly taking my foot off the brake. I studied Jake whenever he drove me anywhere. He looked so good behind the wheel. I could do this. I had to.

The radio was off, as it always was. There was never anything good on the radio. I knew all the quiet side streets that would eventually bring me downtown. Stop signs and traffic circles were less threatening than traffic lights and multiple lanes, and there were far fewer people. My fear and anxiety grew as I got closer to the downtown area, knowing I needed to turn onto the main drag that led to the square. There was so much noise and activity. My body was shaking. I realized I had never taken my pills, as Jake reminded me to do when he left the house.

I spotted Jake's motorcycle parked on the right, just outside the entrance to the bookstore. If I had just come with him. If I had just learned to be at ease on the back of his motorcycle, if I had just been amenable to his interests, this wouldn't be happening. I pulled over just as I saw Jake coming out of the bookstore. I watched him throw his coffee cup in the trash can on the sidewalk and put a package into the side compartment. He looked up, across the intersection.

That was when I saw her. She had long, dark hair, like my mother. She was dressed in a cute white top, faded blue jeans, and heels. I envied women who could pull off jeans with heels. She placed her hand in the air to signal she was crossing the street. Or was she signaling him? I couldn't tell. That's when I saw it, clutched in her hand. Her purse, navy blue and white, in a chevron pattern. Time seemed to slow to a halt. My eyes narrowed as I stared at her, and I swore she looked right at me and smiled. Amused.

My mother sent her. I knew it. She was sent here to punish me for leaving the house. She was sent to take Jake from me. Without another thought, I moved my foot from the brake to the gas and darted into the intersection. I closed my eyes. I didn't care about anyone else on the street. I didn't care about myself. All I cared about was stopping her before she reached him. Before she had a chance to take him from me. He was my soulmate. He belonged to me.

I heard the muffled thud I was waiting for. I paused a few seconds more before opening my eyes, then quickly looked into the rear view mirror, at the crowd gathering around her in the intersection. There. I had found the strength to do what needed to be done.

## TUESDAY MORNING

*Jake*

Hillstrom brought me back to the dark, empty house. I slowly walked through every room on the first floor, looking for anything that belonged to me, or held meaning for me. There was nothing. None of this life had ever been mine.

The steps creaked as I ran upstairs, headed straight for the master bedroom closet. I grabbed my large camping bag from the top shelf and my smaller gym bag from the floor. I took the smaller bag into the bathroom and packed the essentials. Toothbrush, toothpaste, deodorant, body wash, shaving cream, razor, first aid… I realized I was working quickly, anxiously, like I was robbing the place. Once I filled the first bag and zipped it closed, it became real to me. I was getting out of here.

I went back to the closet and set the camping bag on the bench in the center of the wood floor, to pack my clothes. Socks and boxers, t-shirts and jeans, the few of my sweatshirts and sweaters I actually liked, and an extra pair of shoes. I deliberately left all of my work clothes behind. I folded and rolled everything as tightly as I could, just as I had learned as a Boy Scout and practiced on the many camping and hiking trips I'd taken with my brother. Only the nightstand to go.

I opened the nightstand, removed my wedding ring, and left it inside the drawer. Finally, I took Alaina's purse from its hiding place behind the drawer. I held it for a moment, still unable to believe she was really gone. I nestled it into the last bit of open space in the bag. Carrying both bags in one hand, I hurried down the back staircase that came directly into the kitchen. I left my keys on the kitchen counter as I walked out the back door for the very last time.

In the carriage house, I strapped the bags to the tail seat of my motorcycle. I put on my riding gloves, zipped my leather jacket, and slid on my helmet. I swung my right leg over the bike and positioned myself on the cold leather seat. I pulled the heavy machine upright and flipped up the kickstand. The engine's loud growl echoed through the space. The headlight cut through the misty morning fog as I raised the garage door and pulled out of the carriage house.

I knew where I needed to go. I would start my life over in the place she loved most.

It was nearly a straight shot East, from Chicago to upstate New York. It would take about twelve hours or so, not counting the occasional stop to gas up, use the restroom, and stretch my legs. Through Indiana, through Ohio, through Pennsylvania, and then into New York.

I wasn't sure what to expect, once I arrived. I needed to see the family home that meant the world to her. I needed to stand in her mother's garden she kept flourishing after her death. If I could bring myself to unlock the door and step inside her world, would it be just the way I had seen it in my dreams? Would she want me to be there, to stay there, and to be as close to her as I could ever be? I would do that for her. I would do anything for her. I would spend the rest of my life caring for the one place that ever felt like home to her if that was the only way fate would allow me to love her.

Maybe, if I deserved any kind of good fortune, her spirit would settle there and haunt me until I could join her in the afterlife. Suicide wasn't something I'd ever considered, not even on my darkest days. There were so many varying beliefs on what happens to the soul in general, let alone a soul who ended their own life. I couldn't risk, or bear, chasing her for an eternity. I wouldn't want to chance her being reborn without me, and not being able to find her again. I couldn't believe I was even considering these things. The only thing I knew for certain was that if anyone could experience what I had, they would be willing to believe in just about anything.

The first couple of hours went by quickly, with my racing thoughts keeping me thoroughly occupied. I should have been exhausted, but I was wide awake. Wired. The occasional chiming in of the GPS through my helmet, connected to my phone, confirmed I was on the right path.

It started to rain halfway through Ohio. I was pretty well-soaked through by the time I found a roadside motel and pulled over for a while. I brought my bags inside and threw the travel tarp over the bike. A hot shower took away most of the chill, then I climbed into one of the two double beds in the room, my clothes laid out to dry on the other. More exhausted than I realized, I slept straight through to the following morning.

"Go confidently in the direction of your dreams! Live the life you've imagined."

—Henry David Thoreau

## WEDNESDAY MORNING

### Jake

As eager as I was to get there, I didn't mind that I'd delayed my arrival. It was a new day now. It was better somehow not to step into her world on the same day I stepped out of my own. Cleaner. Still tired and my clothes still damp, I packed the bike, shook out the travel tarp, rolled it up tight, and got back on the road.

It wasn't long before I crossed the state line into New York. The final stretch – just another hour or so Northeast. It was more breathtaking than I ever could have imagined. Old farms, vineyards, and serene crystal-clear lakes sprawled the countryside between quaint, picturesque villages. The lush greenery had just begun to make its autumnal turn. I couldn't imagine a more peaceful place to watch the seasons change. I stopped along the side of the road a few times, just to breathe deeply and take it all in, still trying to wrap my mind around where I was now standing compared to where I'd just been. The life that had seemed so inescapable for so long was finally over. I could be anything. I could do anything. For the first time in a long time, my choices were my own.

I rolled up to the welcome sign for Pound Ridge, New York. I didn't need the GPS anymore, I knew my way around. I passed by the places we had been together in my dream. They were all here. They were all real. As I rode through town, I made my initial plans. As soon as I found someplace to stay, I would upgrade my phone and change to a New York number, locate the bookstore, and find the best Americano. I wanted to start hiking, biking, taking nature photographs, and journaling every day.

I was about to turn onto the county road that led to her home. This was it. I slowly turned onto the long, winding driveway and stopped at the top of the hill, removing my sunglasses. There it was, exactly as I'd seen it. Exactly as she'd shown it to me. Her father's garage, her mother's gardens, the house, the courtyard, the pool, and the guest house that became her mother's pottery studio. I walked down the steep pathway into the gardens and stopped to breathe in the scent of the Russian blue sage. Her favorite. I couldn't believe I was standing there. I could feel her all around me, it was as warm and comforting as the afternoon sun following a treacherous and uncomfortable trip.

"Can I help you?"

The question floated toward me, riding the breeze, like music. I knew that voice so well. I looked up and toward the house to see her standing just inside, looking out through the open top of the Dutch door. It couldn't possibly be her. She was gone. I quickly considered all possibilities. *Was she alive and well, or was she gone and I was seeing a ghost? Was I still asleep in the motel and this was my most realistic dream yet? Did I die in a motorcycle crash and this was to be our shared afterlife?* I honestly didn't care which one was true, I was just so relieved to see her.

"Alaina? Is it really you?"

"Yes? Do I know you?"

*No. She didn't know me.* "Hi… My name is Jake Matthews. I have something that belongs to you." I reached into the side compartment of my motorcycle and pulled out her purse, holding it up as I started walking toward her.

She came outside and walked toward me, her arm outstretched, ready to take the purse from me. We reached each other in the center of the garden. She looked up at me and smiled, her eyes were a beautiful blue-gray, just as they were in my dreams.

"Thank you so much for bringing this back to me. I've been lost without it." She shook my hand. "It's a pleasure to meet you, Jake."

"You too," I smiled. I wanted to do so much better than that, but it was all I could manage to say. The energy that had flowed between us when we first met wasn't there now, and I wasn't sure why, but I didn't care. She was standing right in front of me, she still had her life, and I was free to become a part of it.

"Is there any chance you're free tonight? I have an art reception to attend in the early evening, then I thought I'd come home, make a nice dinner, and watch the sunset. Would you like to join me? It's the least I can do to thank you."

"Absolutely," I smiled. "I would love to."

"Then I look forward to seeing you tonight." She turned around and started walking back toward the house, then stopped and turned around again. "You seem so familiar to me. Do you believe in fate, Jake?"

I swung my right leg over the bike and positioned myself on the seat, fidgeting with the temperamental retention strap on my helmet before putting it on. I looked back at her and smiled. "I do now."

"I think hell is something you carry around with you, not somewhere you go." —Neil Gaiman

# WEDNESDAY MORNING

## Alaina

I had the most beautiful dream. A dream I did not want to wake up from. I was at the New York house, with a man I presumed to be my husband, and a darling little girl. We were walking along the beach together on a bright, sunny day. I was walking behind them, wearing my mother's favorite white sundress. The man turned and said something to me with a smile, but I could not hear his words, all I could hear were the waves washing in and out over the golden sand. I could feel the warmth of the sun on my face, chest, and shoulders, and hoped the little girl was wearing enough sunscreen.

*Was this what it was like for my mother when she dreamed of my father after his death?* I understood it now. It felt so real, so heavenly. I'd never given much thought to becoming a wife or a mother, but this dream was enough to make it a consideration. I could feel their love for me, and mine for them. They were moving faster, getting farther and farther ahead of me, as my body seemed to be slowing down. The heavy, wet sand grabbed ahold of my feet, making it increasingly difficult to move forward. *No. Please, no. Don't take me away from them.*

Knowing I was about to regain consciousness, I quickly scanned my mind to be certain I still had all the information I'd gained while asleep. It was all there, from what I could tell. The dreams, the nightmares, the revelations, the conversations with myself. A night had never felt so long before. *Had I astral traveled?* I couldn't be sure what I'd experienced, whether any of it was real or the product of my imagination, but I needed to remember it regardless. I needed to find a good macchiato and a journal, and spend whatever time I had before the art reception getting all of this out of my mind and onto paper before it could slip away. I wished I had my laptop with me. I can type so much more quickly than I can write. This was Chicago, there was bound to be a bookstore and a coffee house nearby. As soon as the weekend was over and I returned to New York, I needed to call Simon and let him know what I'd experienced. He was going to want me in London right away.

The moment I started to raise my eyelids, I snapped them shut and turned my head away from the window. I felt incredibly weak, emaciated, ravenous, and harmed by the sunlight, like some kind of vampire. This was not the quiet, peaceful light of early morning. *Had I overslept? Had I forgotten to close the hotel room curtains?* Both would be highly uncharacteristic of me. I heard a heavy metal cart being rolled down the hallway outside my hotel room. I picked up on the faint smell of disinfectant. If housekeeping was already making their rounds, I had definitely overslept.

I attempted to lift my hands to rub my eyes and reach for my smartphone charging on the nightstand. That was the moment I felt the rough restraining straps around my bare wrists, like worn leather belts, sandpapering the surface of my skin. Panic surged through me. I attempted to move my legs, but my ankles were strapped as well. I blinked frantically to regain clear sight without the assistance of my hands. The bank of windows finally came into focus. There were thick metal bars on them.

This was not my hotel room.

My heart pounded and my breath quickened. The restraints dug into my skin as I struggled against them to free myself. I had somehow gone from unparalleled freedom to radical imprisonment. I'd woken from the most beautiful dream, straight into my worst nightmare.

I looked around the room as my eyes attempted to focus, trying to figure out where I was. It was a small, nearly empty room with one window and two doors. I was lying in a small bed with all white linens. There was a dresser underneath the window and a single chair directly across from the bed, with a framed print of an Andrew Wyeth painting hanging above it. *Christina's World*, 1948. I'd seen the real thing many times at the MOMA in New York. It was a depiction of the young girl who lived next door to Wyeth, who had a degenerative disease that rendered her unable to walk. Refusing to use a wheelchair, she used her upper body to drag herself wherever she desired to go. Wyeth didn't view her as weak or hopeless, he set out to capture her strength and determination. Still, whenever I looked at it, all I saw was how far she was from home, and how long it would take her to get there. I felt sorry for her. But I saw her differently now, as I lay strapped to this bed, determined to free myself at any cost. Immobility is a state of mind.

"Hello?" I shouted toward the door as I tried to release myself from the restraints. The muffled sounds of footsteps and voices echoed through the corridor just outside the door. "Hello? Can anyone hear me?"

*How did I get here? Did I somehow regain consciousness in an alternate universe? How long was I unconscious? Did someone move my body here?* Nothing made sense.

"Hello?" I shouted louder than before.

I strained to peer down at my hands, looking for a way to break free. A second wave of disorientation washed over me. These did not look like my hands. They were disturbingly slender and pale, with short naked fingernails. I was blessed with my mother's glowing olive-toned Mediterranean skin, and I always kept my fingernails long and polished. I worked to bring these foreign fingers as close together as possible and, not without pain, managed to slip them through the left cuff. I could then unbuckle my right wrist, followed by the center strap. I quickly sat up in the bed, instantly feeling nauseous and light-headed. I paused for a moment, telling myself I refused to throw up, then started working to unbuckle my ankles.

I swung my feet over the edge and sat on the side of the bed for a moment, my head lowered and my eyes tightly closed, gripping the side of the mattress edge. I touched my bare feet to the floor. The tile was ice cold. I noticed the pale blue cotton fabric lying just above the bend of my knees. I was wearing a hospital gown. *What was I doing in a hospital?* There was no signage or equipment to otherwise suggest it. No bracelet on my bony wrist. I walked to the closest door and opened it. A bathroom, which I desperately needed to use. Just a toilet and pedestal sink – strangely, with no mirror above it.

After, I walked to the second door, using what little there was in the room to steady me. I took the door handle in both hands and pushed it down. It didn't move. It was locked. Why would I be strapped down and locked in? In rare cases during my consciousness research, a subject would need to be restrained for their own safety, but they were always attached to several non-invasive monitoring devices. They were never left unattended in a locked room.

I stared through the small square window in the door, hoping someone would walk by and see me. Just as I raised my hand to knock on the glass, I gasped as an unfamiliar reflection stared back at me. I touched my face, feeling its strange contours. My mind raced as I struggled to comprehend the startling truth.

It was *her.*
*I* was her.
*How could this happen?*

Part Two

"No mask can be worn forever."

—Morgan Richard Olivier

# TWO YEARS LATER

## Alaina

It had been two years since I awoke within the confines of the Orrington Asylum. Within the confines of Caris Carlisle. For the sake of my sanity, I had done my best to regard this continuation of unfathomable circumstances as a chance to further my consciousness work. When Dex advised me to do something that scared the hell out of me and let it change my life, I sincerely doubted this was what he had in mind.

While working with Simon Kincaid's research group, many of our subjects were found within mental health facilities around the world – people with a variety of abilities and afflictions that their loved ones could not, or would not, understand. Many of those people had opened up to me about the horrific conditions and the inhumane treatments they experienced within the places they were held. Mercifully, the Orrington Asylum was comfortable in comparison to many of those facilities. It was less like a mental hospital and more like a posh rehab center for the rich and famous. This was a place where the privileged hid their unwanted. The patients here were not mistreated, they were simply kept comfortable, quiet, and out of the way. I found gratitude in this, and often reminded myself that it was a far better outcome than serving a prison sentence.

Caris was enough of a prison.

Her mind was a very dark place to reside. Despite the presence of my own consciousness, operating with her disturbed and fragmented mentality was a nightmarish blur of confusion, insecurity, and desperation. This was in addition to the host of concerns that plagued her physical body. As the months wore on, I struggled to maintain my sense of self. I had to constantly remind myself this was happening to her, not to me, and that my presence here was temporary. *It had to be.*

Caris was not allowed phone calls, visitors, or internet access. I knew as long as her father was in control and held authority at this facility, she was never going to be released. The only thing I could do to release myself from Caris was to work toward releasing Caris from herself by overcoming her trauma, overwriting her mindsets, and restoring her overall health. Until she could be deemed fit to be removed from her medication, or trusted enough for it not to be administered under supervision, my consciousness could not leave her body during meditation or sleep.

While my consciousness was very much my own, I was working with what existed in her physical body and mind. I spent the majority of my days combing through her thoughts, attempting to make sense of them. Caris had loved the same man ever since she was a little girl. The way she felt about him reminded me a great deal of my mother and her constant, desperate longing for my father. I was experiencing the way that felt to her, the torment, the anguish of being without the one she loved. I'd never loved someone so much that it consumed me, and until now, I'd always regarded that as a positive.

Her mind rarely strayed from him. I'd come to know Dr. Jake Matthews quite well through her feelings, thoughts, and memories, and I journaled it all – in French. I'd come to find comfort in him, despite not truly knowing him at all. My soul was falling in love with a man I'd never met, based on the way his former wife felt about him. Caris knew her husband was never in love with her, yet he remained tirelessly committed to her, for reasons she had blocked from her conscious mind. She had no knowledge of what became of him, or her family home, when she was involuntarily committed. Only that her wedding ring was gone.

Caris was not allowed to remain nocturnal here. There was a recreational area with a small side room containing a treadmill that took the place of her early morning runs. She was made to eat normal meals, and on a strict schedule, so that her medication could be properly administered. This removed my only opportunity to try to reach anyone who might believe me. It was frustrating, to finally understand how to access the intersection of liminal time and space, but be prevented from doing so. When I dreamed during sleep, it was dreams of Jake, and it was the only time I could behave as my true self. I slept as much as I was allowed to so that I could spend most of my time with him, even though I was not able to actually visit him in those dreams. It was not lost on me that I was coping with my circumstances in the same way my mother had.

My hour-long daily sessions with the asylum's resident psychiatrist were an opportunity to paint Caris in a positive light. After overhearing that she was struggling in her own personal life, I sought to become her friend – not only because we could both use one, but because it was imperative that she not see Caris as a patient needing treatment, but rather as a normal woman who had been wrongfully placed here by her wealthy and powerful father. I told her things about my true self whenever it felt safe to do so. I needed something to be somewhat real to me.

I sat in the familiar leather chair of Dr. Kaitlin's office, a warm light filtering through the tall windows overlooking the front lawn. Sitting here each day, for weeks and months on end, always brought to the surface our only shared subconscious memory – Caris forcibly taking my life from me. Dr. Kaitlin sat in the opposite chair, two cups of coffee on the small round table between us.

"I brought you a caramel macchiato, in honor of your birthday," she smiled.

It wasn't my birthday, it was Caris Carlisle's birthday. "Thank you so much," I replied, truly grateful to savor a taste that brought me back to my true self.

"Of course, happy birthday. I hear you declined your father's phone call this morning."

Charles Carlisle wasn't my father. Lieutenant John James Ryan was my father. Dexter Christian was my father. "Yes, I did."

"Do you want to talk about why?"

"I took his call on my first birthday here. He spent the entire hour talking about himself, how much he was enjoying retirement, and told me all about the young woman he'd been seeing. He didn't even wish his daughter a happy birthday, which was, as I understood it, the reason for the call. I had no desire to sit through that again."

"That was a valid and healthy choice, and it shows a lot of personal growth on your part. I can understand how that would be difficult to hear, given your current circumstances."

"Thank you. May I ask you something?"

"Absolutely."

"Do you think I deserve to be here?"

I knew what Caris had done to me was intentional, she did deserve to be here, but that was a secret we both had to take to the grave.

"No, Caris, I honestly don't. You forgot to take your medication, which in my opinion you no longer need, and it resulted in an unfortunate accident that caused someone minor harm. Had your father not been involved, you would have served maybe nine months in a correctional facility, and probably a fine for driving without a license, and that's it."

The following morning, I heard a string of words I thought I might never hear for the rest of my life.

"Ms. Carlisle, you have a visitor."

This was an interesting development that gave me an injection of hope. I hadn't seen a soul that wasn't employed by the asylum for the last two years. I leaped from the chair I had moved next to the window where the dresser used to be and hurried to the adjoining bathroom to pull myself together. Once I managed to convince them I was not a danger to myself, they afforded me a mirror above the sink. In the absence of any makeup, I pinched her cheeks to add a bit of color to her pale but flawless complexion. I brushed through her straight blonde hair, which was now quite long, and tied it back in a simple low ponytail. It wasn't my style, but Caris liked her hair pulled back and neat.

The aide waiting outside my door escorted me to the solarium. The solarium was my sanctuary here, aside from my hour each day with Dr. Kaitlin. Caring for the plants brought joy to my soul and allowed me to feel like my true self. There wasn't much to work with initially, but I'd been allowed to make a list of seedlings and propagation tools to expand it. I could close my eyes and imagine I was at home in Pound Ridge, tending to my mother's gardens. I hoped that if Caris had been living my life for the last two years, she was at least taking care of my home as if it were her own.

I prayed that it would be anyone from my own life, not someone from hers. Anyone at all, knowing full well what an unrealistic prayer that was. I saw the back of a man standing at the other end of the room, looking out the windows. He turned around and smiled as I approached. I didn't know him, in either life.

"Ms. Carlisle, my name is David Hillstrom. I've worked for your father for many years. May we sit?"

"Yes, of course."

We turned two large dark brown wicker chairs that faced the windows to face each other. He sank into the deep chair, grunting as he leaned back and rested his arms on the sides. He brought his hand to his bottom lip, pinching it in hesitation, then ran his fingers along his short beard, from cheeks to chin.

"I'm afraid I have some bad news. Your father passed away yesterday afternoon. He had a heart attack on the golf course." He paused for my reaction, and I had to feign a degree of sorrow for a man I didn't know or care about. "This dissolves his power of attorney over both you and your mother, as well as his seat on the board of directors here. A court-appointed representative spoke with the hospital administrator and the rest of the board this morning, and it's been decided that your mother will remain here as a ward of the state."

"And what will happen to me?"

"I'm not sure if you were aware of this, but your father had remarried. His most recent will indicated the whole of his assets were to be transferred to his new wife and their infant son. Mrs. Carlisle has stated she will not continue to fund your care, effective immediately. The good news is that the hospital administrator deferred to the expertise of your psychiatrist, who sees no reason to make you a ward of the state. Your release documents are being prepared as we speak, and your personal effects are being retrieved from storage. I'm here to take you anywhere you want to go. The bad news is that your family home was sold two years ago, and you don't have a dime."

Sitting in the passenger seat of Mr. Hillstrom's car, I removed the lid from the small box that contained her personal effects. Her phone, her wallet, and her keys. I couldn't help but laugh. I'd always said that as long as I had these three things, I was secure in an insecure world. Her phone was deactivated, her wallet was empty, and her keys were to a house that was no longer hers.

"Look… I worked for your father for a long time. He was good to me, and I was loyal to him. I've already been paid through the month, so why don't we just say I work for you for the time being, alright? Where can I take you?"

"Meridian Gallery."

"May you never go back to the dark places you fought so hard to get out of." —Unknown

TWO YEARS LATER

## Jake

I never went back to Chicago. I left it in the past where it belonged. Pound Ridge was a welcomed change of pace and scenery. I loved being a groundskeeper, working alone and for myself, and having plenty of spare time to hike, bike, and run. I took up nature photography. The independent bookstore in town had a modest coffee bar that made a passable Americano.

I fully expected to be starting over on my own, and maybe that's exactly what I should have done. The feeling that overcame me when I first met Alaina was completely absent now, and I didn't understand why. Maybe that amazing feeling solely exists to let us know when we've encountered our soulmate, and once we have that knowledge, the feeling fades away. Maybe everything she went through changed her. *How could it not?* Maybe everything I went through with Caris changed me. I had more questions than answers.

Alaina had all the outward appearances of the woman I'd fallen in love with. She had no recollection of the hit and run, and she had no memory of the dreams we shared while she was in the coma. That I could live with. That was understandable. It made medical sense. But I began to notice many subtle inconsistencies over time, occasional concerning behavior had become more frequent, and I hated to say it, but she began to show traces of instability that reminded me so much of Caris. Maybe that was karma at work.

I thought I had finally found peace and contentment with the literal woman of my dreams, following a turbulent and toxic marriage. As I replayed the last two years in my mind, I searched for signs that I somehow might have missed, and questioned how I could have been so blind. I was taken right back to feeling trapped in a relationship I didn't want, in a home that wasn't my own, longing for the woman I couldn't have.

Only now, we were expecting a child.

TWO YEARS LATER

*Caris*

The last two years were the best of my life. Jake and I had the fresh start I had always wanted for us, that I never believed was possible. This time, he was in love with me. This time, I was in love with myself.

Within Alaina, I had come to life. I flourished. I was beautiful, healthy, and strong, not to mention younger. I had her knowledge, memories, mindsets, habits, talents, and skills – all of which provided me with a blueprint for ideal living. She wasn't limited by her challenges and adversities, they fueled her. I finally had the chance to study art, and I began using her mother's old studio to develop a daily practice.

No longer taking the pills that kept my mind still, my consciousness was able to travel anywhere I wished to go, during both sleep and meditation. I constantly returned to Alaina's body with new knowledge and abilities. I studied all of the research her laptop and journals held, and began adding my own findings to it. It became an obsession.

Before long, it became impossible to discern where she ended and I began.

I awoke to the sight of a white coffered ceiling, instantly wondering what kind of monster would paint historic woodwork. I lay on my back in bed, fully clothed, and above the covers. The back of my neck throbbed where the gathering point of my ponytail pressed into it. I lifted my hands, which had been clasped in front of me, and raised them into my line of vision. Pale hands with short naked nails. Hands I forgot had once been mine. My wedding ring was gone.

Looking around me, I realized I was in a hotel room. I sprung from the bed and peered into the large mirror that hung above the credenza. I slowly dragged my fingers down my face in disbelief. My consciousness had returned to my former self. *Why was this happening?* I had complete control of where I traveled, and I would never have chosen to return to my former body and life. I considered the possibility that there was a time limit and I had reached it.

I ran my hands down my arms, then across my stomach. I'd never thought of myself as ugly before. I used to believe I was plain, but pretty. My face and body were perfectly symmetrical, and my skin was flawless. I stayed fit, and I dressed well. It had been a delusion that my outward appearance disguised the darkness that resided within me. Looking at myself now, I was able to see the truth. I was able to see myself the way Jake always had. The way my parents had. I was a monster.

I noticed something in the mirror and quickly spun around. A large window with a window seat, overlooking the cliffs at the edge of the property. This was not a hotel room. This was the master bedroom of my family home. A home that now belonged to someone else, and I was trespassing. In a panic, I rushed to the door and peeked out, trying to determine if the house was empty. I hurried down the upstairs hallway and crept down the main staircase, crouched down as if it made me any less visible. It reminded me of when I was a little girl, trying to sneak downstairs during my parents' parties. I paused at the base of the stairs and looked around for a moment. Everything had been changed. The woodwork had all been painted white, the vintage wallpapers removed, and the walls painted light neutral colors. The furnishings were modern and subdued, which should have felt wrong surrounded by heavy historical mill-work and detailing, but somehow they made it work – a dichotomy this house was quite familiar with. There didn't seem to be anyone home. I quietly made my way through the first floor rooms and into the kitchen. There was a vase of fresh flowers in the center of the island, just as there had always been. Next to it, there sat a book. I opened it to find pages and pages of names and addresses. A guestbook. My family home was now a bed and breakfast. A revolving door of goddamn strangers. I slammed the book shut in disgust.

I heard the front door open. I hurried out the back door, through the garden, and ducked into the greenhouse. I curled up in the large wicker chair in the corner and covered my legs with the throw blanket that was draped over it. It began to rain. Through the clouds of greenery, I had a narrow view of the house. Not so long ago it was the only place that could ever feel like home to me, and now I barely recognized it. I barely recognized myself.

"Ms. Carlisle?"

I opened my eyes to realize I was still in the greenhouse, and still restored to my original factory settings. A man I presumed to be the present owner of my family home was peering down at me with pity and concern in his eyes.

"Ms. Carlisle, are you alright? Did you sleep out here?"

"I must have," I replied blearily, attempting to hide my anger in realizing I had once again woken up in this life. I had truly hoped this was some sort of glitch, a wrong turn, a bad dream, and I would wake up this morning back where I belonged, next to my husband.

"You received a package. It's waiting for you in the kitchen, along with your breakfast."

I wasn't trespassing. Alaina must have checked into the bed and breakfast to leave my body here. I couldn't decide whether that was considerate or cruel. I followed the man back to the kitchen and sat down at the table in front of a plate of blueberry ricotta pancakes. I pushed the plate away from me and grabbed the large manila envelope next to it. I pulled out a lengthy document with a letter fastened to the front of it, in my own handwriting. I looked inside the envelope for any other contents, finding a set of keys at the bottom and pouring them out onto the table.

*Caris,*

*If you're reading this, that means I have managed to correct what you have done. I have been trapped within my own body, then trapped within yours, and then trapped a third time within the Orrington Asylum – all at your hands. I had no choice but to get to know you well, as I spent two long and painful years sorting through the darkest caverns of your mind and heart. While I will never condone your actions, I will admit I have come to understand them. To understand you.*

*I wish I could say I'm sorry to inform you of your father's death, but it's the only reason I was released. Your mother will remain there as a ward of the state until her death. Your father's holdings now belong to his widow and their infant son.*

*I believe I owe you some modicum of thanks. Your actions have brought about understandings I otherwise might not have reached, which have changed both my life and my work, and I am eager to return to both. I'm sure you're already aware that Dexter has decided to retire. As outlined in the enclosed document, Meridian Gallery now belongs to you. I am not able to leave you with nothing, as you did me. This will be the final thing you acquire at my expense.*

*Alaina Ryan*

I rummaged through the desk in the library and returned to my room with stationery, a pen, and a stamped envelope. I had my own letter to write. That night I roamed the halls, just as I used to. The ghosts and shadows welcomed me home. New ownership and a fresh coat of paint weren't enough to drive them away.

In the early morning, when darkness faded but the sun had not yet risen, I went for a run. The ghosts and shadows of the night followed the darkness home, but the living world had not yet begun to stir. I focused on the sound of my labored breaths, aligned with the echoing thumps of my running shoes against the pavement. I worked my way through the maze of cul-de-sacs that made up our neighborhood, lined with similar imposing manors behind tall iron gates.

I ended my run at the back of the property, standing on the edge of the cliff, looking down at the unforgiving path to the bottom. I would take one step backward from the edge for each thing I could find to be grateful for, knowing full well that the day I could no longer find a reason to take a step backward would be the day I took a step forward.

I closed my eyes, held my breath, and took a step forward.

*Dear Jake,*

*As you move forward without me as your wife in this lifetime, please choose to remember everything we shared in our final two years. It may not have been my mind and body, but it was my soul. We ultimately found happiness together, and you cannot deny that.*

*I have no regrets. I have always, and will always, find a way to be with you at any cost. You are my soulmate. Together we will have countless beginnings and no ending. You are eternally and rightfully mine.*

*Exactly when a fetus acquires consciousness is not medically known. While an unborn child can react to touch, sound, and pain, these reactions are thought to be of subcortical, nonconscious origin. They may also be partially comatose due to endogenous sedation and low oxygen levels. Most data suggests that consciousness emerges near 24 weeks of gestation, once thalamocortical connections are established.*

*We will meet again soon, and I know that you will love me.*

*Caris*

# Epilogue
The French White Notebook


Poterie en Céramique
*pour ma fille, Alaina*


Ma Fille Chérie,

C'est à la hâte, à la fin de ma vie, que je crée ces œuvres. Je les crée pour toi, pour dire les nombreuses choses que je n'ai pas su dire. J'ai cru qu'il fallait sacrifier mon âme de créatrice pour être ta mère. En vérité, tu es ma plus belle création.

Ta Mère Aimante



Ceramic Pottery
*For my daughter, Alaina*


*My Darling Girl,*

*It is with haste at the end of my life that I create these works. I create them for you, to say the many things I have failed to say. I thought that I needed to sacrifice my creative soul to be your mother. In truth, you are my most beautiful creation.*

*Your Loving Mother*

# Postface

Coma patients often experience a range of strange and mysterious occurrences, both during their time in a coma and after they emerge from it. These experiences vary widely from person to person, but some of these unusual experiences include:

Lucid Dreams and False Memories:

Some coma patients report having vivid, lifelike dreams or hallucinations that feel entirely real. These dreams can be confusing and may involve interactions with people who are not present or events that never occurred.

Out-of-Body Experiences:

Some individuals in comas or near-death experiences claim to have had out-of-body experiences. They describe a sensation of floating above their own bodies, observing the medical staff and their surroundings from a different perspective.

Time Distortion:

Coma patients sometimes report experiencing a distorted sense of time. What feels like hours or even days to them might only be minutes or seconds in the real world.

Encounters with Deceased Loved Ones:

Some patients report encounters with deceased loved ones during their coma state. They describe conversations or interactions with deceased friends or family members, which can be comforting or unsettling.

Sensory Perceptions:

Patients may perceive sensory stimuli while in a coma, such as hearing voices, sounds, or feeling touch. These perceptions may or may not correspond to actual events in the hospital room.

Tunnel Experiences:

Similar to near-death experiences, some coma patients describe a sensation of traveling through a tunnel or corridor toward a bright light. This phenomenon is often associated with a feeling of peace and tranquility.

Emotional Resonance:

Coma patients may report strong emotional experiences, such as intense feelings of fear, love, or happiness. These emotions can be triggered by their dreams, hallucinations, or sensory perceptions.

Incomplete Memories:

When patients begin to emerge from a coma, they may have fragmented or incomplete memories of their experiences. They may struggle to distinguish between what was real and what was part of their coma-induced dreams or hallucinations.

Difficulty Communicating:

Even after regaining consciousness, some coma patients may have difficulty communicating their experiences due to physical limitations or cognitive impairment.

Post-Traumatic Stress:

Some patients who have experienced strange or distressing phenomena during their coma may develop symptoms of post-traumatic stress disorder (PTSD) after awakening, particularly if their experiences were frightening or disorienting.

These experiences are highly subjective and may not be universally shared among coma patients. The scientific understanding of these phenomena is limited, and researchers continue to study and explore the mysteries of human consciousness, including astral travel and the possibility of alternate realities.

In addition to modern gothic fiction novels, EL Block also writes short stories, flash fiction, and poetry. Her most notable works include *American Gothic*, *Monstera*, and *The Last American Vampire*.

Connect online: @elblockauthor

OTHER NOVELS BY EL BLOCK
*Available through all major booksellers.*

American Gothic (2022)      978-1-955047-04-3 (paperback)
                            978-1-955047-05-0 (eBook)

Monstera (2023)            978-1-955047-34-0 (paperback)
                            978-1-955047-47-0 (eBook)

# Soulmate Playlist
Available on Spotify

| | |
|---|---|
| Make It Without You | Andrew Belle |
| Daylight | David Kushner |
| Stubborn Love | The Lumineers |
| So In Love With You | Jake Etheridge |
| Light In My Eyes | The Last Revel |
| To Build A Home | The Cinematic Orchestra / Patrick Watson |
| Into The Mystic | Van Morrison |
| I've Got Dreams To Remember | Otis Redding |
| All I Want Is You | U2 |
| Turning Page | Sleeping At Last |
| Home | Edith Whiskers |
| Nothing Was Stolen | Phosphorescent |
| Never Tear Us Apart | Bishop Briggs |
| Home | Matthew Hall |
| This House | Matthew Hall |
| Where's My Love | SYML |
| Only For You | Heartless Bastards |
| Dreams | The Cranberries |
| Goodbye My Lover | James Blunt |
| This Year's Love | David Gray |

"This isn't it," she whispered.